Advance Praise for *Into the Woods*

"David Wood has crafted a gem of a story laced with action, villainy, revenge and reconciliation. Adventure, loyalty — sometimes strained and split, love, and sacrifice resonate within the pages of this historical fiction tale."
Terry W. Ervin II, author of *Flank Hawk,* a First Civilization's Legacy novel

Praise for David Wood's *Cibola*

"Ancient cave paintings? Cities of gold? Secret scrolls? Sign me up! *Cibola* is a twisty tale of adventure and intrigue that never lets up and never lets go!"
Robert Masello, author *of Blood and Ice*, *Vigil*, and *Bestiary*

"With the thoroughly enjoyable way Mr. Wood has mixed speculative history with our modern day pursuit of truth, he has created a story that thrills and makes one think beyond the boundaries of mere fiction and enter the world of 'why not'? *Cibola* is a worthy tale!"
David Lynn Golemon, Author of *Event, Legend, Ancients,* and *Leviathan*

"*Cibola* by David Wood is a page-turning yarn blending high action, Biblical speculation, ancient secrets, and nasty creatures. Indiana Jones better watch his back!"
Jeremy Robinson, author of *Kronos* and *Antarktos Rising*

"History is turned on its head in this gripping tale of sects, secrets, and double-crosses. With mesmerizing treasures in beautiful locations, beautiful women and rugged heroes, mysticism and mystery, Wood spins a yarn that keeps the pages turning."
Alan Baxter, author of *RealmShift* and *MageSign*

Praise for David Wood's *Dourado*

"*Dourado* is a brisk read, reminiscent of early Cussler adventures, and perfect for an afternoon at the beach or a cross-country flight. You'll definitely want more of Maddock."
Sean Ellis, author of *The Shroud of Heaven*

"*Dourado* is a fast-paced adventure with action to spare. Dane Maddock is a hero cut from the Dirk Pitt mold, and "Bones" Bonebrake is the best sidekick around. If you like your thrillers with a touch mystery and Biblical archaeology, *Dourado* is the book for you."
Megalith Book Reviews

"Mr. Wood has crafted an amazing story that combines adventure, faith, history and excitement in equally fascinating measure. I'm looking forward to reading the next in the series."
Xanthorpe Reviews

Other Works by David Wood

Dourado
Cibola

Acknowledgements:

The authors would like to thank the following people for their invaluable assistance in making this book a reality:

Cindy Baker
Cara Ballard
Alan Baxter
Barbara Blake
Susan Boswell
Sean Ellis
Terry W. Ervin II
Kristy Gleaton
Zebrina Warner

INTO THE WOODS

DAVID WOOD
DAVID S. WOOD

Gryphonwood

Gryphonwood Press

Published by Gryphonwood Press
www.gryphonwoodpress.com

This book is a work of fiction. All names, characters,
places and incidents are the product of the author's
imagination, or are used fictitiously. Any resemblance to
actual events or persons is entirely coincidental.

ISBN: 0-9825087-2-7
ISBN 13:   978-0-9825087-2-5
Printed in the United States of America
First printing: December, 2009

This book is dedicated to the memory of
Jonathan Wood, and that of all the
courageous people who settled
"Over the Mountains."

Prologue

The dying man's words made little sense to Bear Heart. With his final, strained breaths, the man had whispered to Bear Heart about secrets and danger and the white man's god. Bear Heart thought there was also something about Croatoan. Of course, he might have misunderstood some of what the man had said. His English was as imperfect as his memory.

Of this much, he was certain: the dying man wanted the information on this piece of paper kept safe. Safe from whom, he had not said. How it should be done was also a mystery.

He looked down at the stranger. His hair was cut short—not like the Englishmen he had met. His clothing was odd as well: a black, hooded cloak worn over garments of the same black. His boots were worn, but had obviously belonged to a man of wealth. His hands were marked with symbols, the likes of which Bear Heart had never seen. Around his neck hung a thick, silver chain upon which was suspended another symbol of some sort. Bear Heart assumed it was an item of power, so he dared not touch it.

The man also carried a pack, but its contents were ordinary. Bear Heart ignored the metal circles the white men called "coins." An Indian who tried to trade with them would be accused of thievery. The man would no longer have need of his blanket, his knife, or his dried meat, so Bear Heart took those. He found a jar of the burning liquid that brought the good dreams and took it as well.

A raven peered down from a low-hanging limb, scolding him with its harsh call.

"You be quiet," Bear Heart chided. "I imagine you might feast on the dead from time-to-time yourself." The raven squawked again and took wing, leaving Bear Heart smiling at its receding form. He had gotten the better of that argument. Oh yes he had!

He buried the man in the soft ground where a massive, ancient tree had fallen. The stump had decayed over the years, leaving a circle of black dirt which crumbled in Bear Heart's palm, thick with the pungent scent of earth. A white man with a strange accent had once told him that such places were visited by spirit folk. Perhaps the man would have company in death.

He covered the grave over with stones to protect it from predators. He knew that white men said words over their dead, but he did not know what those words were, and he felt he had already done enough for this stranger. Tonight, the owls would sing a song of mourning for this fallen intruder into Bear Heart's land.

Now, what to do with this secret?

He thought about it for a long while as he walked. A slow thinker, Bear Heart was better with his bow than his mind, but given sufficient time, he usually came up with a reasonable solution to any problem.

After many steps and few ideas, he sat down on a rocky ledge overlooking a valley of green. The rock was cool under his skin and the clean air seemed to sharpen his mind. He chewed on a piece of dried meat, letting the juices of his mouth release the flavor, and thought some more.

The man had not told him to destroy the paper. In fact, the man could have destroyed it himself. Obviously, the secret needed to be preserved, but in a way that it could be kept safe. But safe from whom remained the nagging question.

He would have to hide the paper. There was no other way to keep it secure. But there was another problem. Paper such as this did not last. How could he preserve it? Carving it into stone would take much too long. He supposed he could paint it onto a cave wall, but he was much better at carving. He scratched his head, as if to jar the ideas into motion. He let his hand trail through his thick, black hair, and his fingers touched the leather thongs that held his gorget in place.

His gorget! He could carve the lines from this paper onto the back of his shell gorget. That would preserve them. And he knew of a perfect cave nearby where he could hide it. It was not the sort of place in which a hunter would pass the night—just a small spot into which he had ducked once when trying to avoid detection by enemy warriors. He doubted anyone else had ever bothered with it. He smiled a satisfied smile. He always came up with a plan.

The sun was low on the horizon as Bear Heart made his way down off of the mountain. He was well pleased with himself. The white man's secret was in a safe place, but also preserved so that it would not be lost. What would become of it now? That was none of his concern.

Chapter 1

September, 1763

The rocky promontory looked out over a lush valley. The crisp, evening breeze carried the tangy scent of rain across the outcropping. Autumn's brush had touched lightly along ridgelines, bronzing the hardwoods. Her next stroke would bleed scarlet against the golds and purples. The far distant peaks seemed to merge into a rolling sea of dark blue. With a touch of melancholy Jonathan gazed across the hollows of the Moccasin Valley. Even from the heights, he could hear the moving water of a narrow, winding creek. Back home, in the Tidewater, creeks were broad, slow, dark, and soundless. Here in this valley, Moccasin Creek was alive, wending its way between the mountains with a vigor befitting its namesake, drawn westward by the last rays of the evening sun. The reverence with which his father had always spoken of the works of God settled into his bones as he surrendered to the timeless scene that lay before him.

Another feeling came to him, unbidden and unexpected into his heart: envy. He longed to be a twig swept along by the insistent current, carried beyond the next hill and into the unknown. He had a sudden image of this verdant valley, with its rich, black soil, stately trees, and abundant life all being pulled away, washing eternally westward. His panicked heart urged him to follow, for every step he had taken into this broad expanse of wilderness seemed to bring him closer to a home he never knew he had lost.

His work was nearly finished, and he would begin the trip home the following day. He could not help but envy Dr. Walker's foresight in having seen the potential value of the high ridge and valley region of Virginia. Thomas Walker had the backing and connections to form the Loyal Land Company and obtained this enormous grant. Jonathan and his crew had spent weeks surveying claims for settlers. There were no whites to be seen now but a few had already been there, marking trees with their axes, building rude shelters, planting corn, all to "prove up" their claim. Jonathan gave his mind free rein to wonder. Perhaps he himself could...

No, there was too much holding him back there — too many reasons that kept him east of the

Blue Ridge. Land agents back in Williamsburg had uncovered some obscure details of the terms of a new treaty with the Indians. In exchange for peace, King George was to have established a line down the Blue Ridge across which no white man could settle or even hunt. If this were true, only Indians could live across these mountains.

Jonathan knew, however, that the Crown's governor could read between the lines, and had turned his eyes away from the flood of settlers pouring down the great valley of Virginia. Governor Berkeley knew that the best way to defend the rich tidewater plantations of the east was to have whites settle across the Blue Ridge to bear the brunt of the inevitable attacks by Indians. He also knew that the vast majority of these settlers would consist of the hard-bitten Scots-Irish, clannish types who, even now, were moving south on the Great Philadelphia Wagon Road.

As the setting sun began to seal his thoughts of this closing day, Jonathan felt a shadow of regret descend upon him. Civilization, as some termed it, was neither for him, nor he for it. His father might see things differently, but, at home, Jonathan felt... stagnated, constricted. Surveying had afforded him some of that which he craved, but each taste of virgin territory only served to whet his appetite and sharpened his longing to a fine edge. Something had to change.

The chilled darkness finally drove him deep into the warmth of his horsehair blanket. Wrapped in its rough folds and his own discontent, he settled into an uneasy slumber.

The following day quickly became one of contradictions. His journal of tracts was current, the chain and rod crew had already started home, yet he found himself lingering at every turn of the trail. Mornings in the forest were loud for those who knew the origin of every sound. The animals that labored by day spent every waking moment in search of sustenance. Jonathan had often contemplated a mind that never wandered but stayed steadily on the task at hand. Nevertheless, there was now stillness as he walked, a stillness that lingered far longer than his stride as he moved past the ferns and thick laurel. Survival for creatures of the woodland depended on constant motion, stopping only when danger threatened.

Someone or something was behind him and had been all day. Animals of prey, the catamount or packs of wolves tended to attack by dark when they had advantage. Still yet, the sunlight slanted some. If harm were to come, the opportunity was fast approaching.

Jonathan, though of a contemplative turn, could not abide inaction when danger threatened. He followed an ancient belief that the harder the storm, the quicker it passed. His eyes scanned the surrounding area one last time. He had heard that the forests of this land were so dense that a squirrel could leap branch to limb, tree to tree, from Montreal to St. Augustine without ever having to touch the ground, and it was true. Nothing was visible in this dense wood. A glimmer of green and gold to his right indicated a clearing, and he seemed to dare an attack by passing directly through. Yet there was method in his act, for he muffled his own sounds by stepping only on rocks or fallen trees. He knew of attacks betrayed by some sound that was off key from the timeless hymn of the forest. Any rustle of leaves or snap of a twig could signal the predator's intention.

The late afternoon passed in such ploys until he doubted there was cause for fear. Night came quickly in the hills. If your path was deep in the hollow, it seemed the sun just sank without giving sign of its leaving. He lay down his rifle and budget pack at the edge of the stream that poured through the bottomland.

He pitched a camp beneath a large river birch tree. In this spot, the water slowed and formed an oxbow. He unwound his fishing gear and searched for bait under a rotting log, until his efforts were rewarded with a fat grub, which he put on his hook. Swinging the line above his head, he cast over the deep, clear pool just as the sun struck the tops of the tall pines. He almost immediately felt a tug and heard the satisfying splash of a fish on the line.

He set about making a small cook fire, shielding it behind a screen of wide strips of bark, woven between short stakes to hide its glow from searching eyes. The light of a few small flames would not penetrate this dense forest. He had not seen a soul since his crew led the packhorses away, yet he still sensed a presence that was unmistakably human. He knew this to be the shared hunting ground of a number of the Shawnee, Cherokee, and Mingo tribes, as well as the occasional path of a French trapper or long hunter. An honest measure of caution, with a touch of enticement, would serve him well. He allowed a mite of err to poise as a lure for an incautious attack.

He cleaned the fat bluegill he had caught, here, in Moccasin Creek. Using his flint and some curly birch bark, he ignited the bits of tinder, adding twigs, and soon sticks of hardwood as the flames grew. He then skewered the fish and set it over the fire where it crackled and sizzled. Ideally, he would have let the fire burn down to coals before cooking, but he did not want to keep the flames burning any longer than necessary. The aroma wafted through the air, teasing his nose and setting his stomach to growling. The ease with which he had landed the fish, snaring it with the grub on a bone hook and a length of twine, still amazed him. It was as if the fish wanted to jump right out of the water and into his belly.

A flash of movement at the corner of his eye drew his attention. It was no more than a flitting shadow, but it was enough. Knowing beforehand that his long barreled rifle was a weapon of intent rather than reaction, he gripped his skinning knife. Jonathan's knife hand was as good at throwing as it was at thrusting. Not a sound warned him of his adversary's advance. He knew, as if by instinct, that his stalker's intent was to show scorn for Jonathan's strategy rather than to do him bodily harm.

A tall, lean figure melted out of the darkness. Plainly, a Cherokee, hair plucked, buckskin breech-cloth, knife tucked in his beaded belt, and a trade hatchet tied with a leather thong. His hands were open and extended as a sign of peace. A finely dressed strap of leather held an ancient flintlock musket across his back. The gun was of Spanish origin, probably traded many times on its path from Florida to the Cherokee towns.

"You hide your flame well for an English," he said. "I tired of tracking you. Almost abandoned the play until the scent of your fire led me to seek one who made to tempt Duwalla."

Jonathan nodded. The Indian seemed to carry no ill intent beyond proving himself the better woodsman. Jonathan's posture belied his mindful caution by motioning for the man to join him at the fire, and then settling uneasily to the ground. The Indian dropped down onto the balls of his feet on the other side of the fire.

"Fish?" Jonathan offered, taking the skewer from over the flames.

"My thanks," the Indian said. He dipped a hand into his tipi bag and pulled out a small, wrapped bundle. "Fry bread," he explained, pulling out what looked like hoecakes and handing one to Jonathan.

Jonathan balanced the bread on his thigh and, with a deft stroke, sliced off a chunk of fish and dropped it onto the bread. He did the same for the other man. The Indian nodded and accepted this act as penitence for the temerity of testing Duwalla's dominance. Dropping comfortably to the ground, he seemed to mock any fear of this young man being a threat to him.

Jonathan took a bite of the fish and bread. The bluegill had a strong flavor and the bread was chewy but not altogether bad. Certainly not as dry and crumbly as corn pone.

As they ate in silence, he thought how strange it would seem to his family back in the Tidewater, that he would be breaking bread with a "savage" who might kill him at any moment. They would never understand the subtle signs between two men that indicated peace or the threat of violence. Staring at the waning flames of the tiny cook fire, he found the quiet to be comforting. His father had never failed to fill any gap in conversation, whether or not he had something of consequence to say. Jonathan, however, was not much for words unless he had something to share.

He washed his meal down with a swig of water from his flask. He offered a drink to the Indian, who accepted gratefully. Now that they had shared food and drink, it seemed to Jonathan as good a time as any to break the silence.

"Name's Wood. Jonathan Wood," he said. He did not offer his hand, as he would have to an Englishman. "I'm a surveyor from up above the Shenandoah."

The Indian inclined his head. "My name is Duwalla of Tomotley in the lower towns."

"You speak the English quite well," Jonathan observed, hoping Duwalla would take that as a compliment rather than an assumption that all Indians were mutes.

"As good as Jonathan Wood?" Duwalla asked, with an aura of contention mixed with tolerance. "Father taught me some. Learned more from a long hunter I scouted with years ago. Now I visit the white settlements enough that I speak it better than most. I spend a lot of time on the Kanawha, where you call the New River." He paused for a time, gazing into the dark. "If you are a surveyor," he finally said, "that means more whites think to settle here." It was a statement, not a question, so Jonathan simply nodded and kept his silence.

"They are not welcome here," Duwalla said. Jonathan was not surprised, but indignation must have shown on his face. "It is not that I hate the English," Duwalla added. "Many pass through here to hunt. Others simply pass through. It is shared land. No one makes a home here — especially not the English. The French come and leave with only the skins of the creatures, but the English take the skin of the land."

"They will come regardless," Jonathan said. It was the simple truth. When the hunger for more land and breathing room took hold of a man, the dangers were pushed to some far place in his mind. He had not understood that until coming to this valley. Now it had taken hold of him. "I might even settle here myself." He said it without thinking, but he knew it had become a desire unlikely to be set aside.

"I wish you good range and shelter, but mind Duwalla's words. Blood has marked this as ground no man may hold in his hand. When it flows anew, let it not be yours." The words did not chill Jonathan, as they probably should. His mind was set. He would call this land his own.

Jonathan broke camp at daybreak and as expected, Duwalla was already gone. Jonathan could plainly see Duwalla's tracks headed southwest to the Big Moccasin Gap. The gap revealed the tireless work of the swift running creek giving proof of God's intention. Here, the seemingly impenetrable range of Clinch Mountain had been worn down nearly level. Soon, it would be widened by the axe even more than the passage of endless bison herds or the footfalls of innumerable travelers. But on this day, the rocky, southwestern face of Clinch Mountain blocked the light of the morning sun rising in the east. The narrow path and the dark shade could hide unseen danger. The rushing stream was louder, still knifing through the mountain's break. If God intended this place as a helping passage to the western lands, His unknowable will offered it also as a test of a man's courage and caution. The gap's steep, northern face, strewn with boulders and giant pines, offered any man with ill intent an opportunity to ambush even the most vigilant.

Jonathan followed Duwalla's tracks, trusting those moccasin prints would follow the best and safest path. Duwalla's path forded the creek and then passed through a grove of hardwoods. Standing at the crest, Jonathan saw the mouth of the Big Moccasin Gap. Evergreens climbed the face of Clinch Mountain, which seemed to incline suggesting a sleeping giant. Feeling secure with following Duwalla's way, he quickened his pace and lengthened his stride. If Duwalla intended to go north and follow the ancient Warriors' Path, Jonathan would lose this advantage. His journey would take him south through the gap, then northeast.

After many days, he would make his way back to the South Branch of the Potomac. He looked forward to passing through the great valley of Virginia. On this day, however, he must still be aware of his every step and every sound. Reaching the lowest point of the gap, he again had to ford the creek, but here it narrowed, white water rushing loudly around his legs.

Here in the deep shade of the gap's laurel, with the water drowning out all other sounds, he began to feel a sense of danger that he had not felt on his journey. He now questioned his decision to send the crew on ahead. He knew the Indian leaders had agreed to peace. The true danger came, not from the leaders, but from the renegades, those enticed by the French agents operating out of Detroit. These men ranged from the Great Lakes to Florida, trading weapons and rum for the plunder that raiding bands took from the settlers. The most valuable objects of plunder were the slaves, who were sent down the Mississippi and sold in the markets of New Orleans. White women and children were held for ransom in Detroit. Although horses were rare in the mountains, a few could be found in the Shenandoah Valley and brought the thieves a good return among the traders north of the Ohio.

His wariness was honed to a fine edge by a restless night, due to the abiding uncertainty of Duwalla's intentions, and the fact that he had not eaten since the night before did not help. His best course was to put his worries aside and maintain a pace that could allow him to ford the Holston River and find shelter before sunset.

He ascended a ridge so steep that he had to walk a meandering angle to reach the top. The exertion was worth it, for here he could see the breadth of the valley he had just traversed. The north led to a hollow, walled in by the Clinch Mountain and the ridge upon which he now stood. He could see the hollow actually open to a valley choked by a dense pine forest. Experience had taught him that pine lands indicated soil of poor vigor. Looking to the south, he saw the richness of the lower Moccasin Valley. Old Indian fields were still evident from the lack of virgin forest along the creek bank. The slight rise of the land held treasure, for here, under the watchful eye of the Clinch Mountain's rocky face, stood a mound. This small knoll was not of God's hands alone but had risen by the work of a people so ancient that even to the elders of the Cherokee they were a mystery.

Descending the piney ridge, he heard the chatter of fox squirrels and then he saw the north fork of the Holston. It was wide and shallow at this point. He forded here where the water was only knee deep. Unlike Moccasin Creek, it still held some warmth from the past summer's sun. The path now wound over low hills and through a gap so narrow that two packhorses abreast could not have passed.

The way became rocky, but then opened to a wide green valley. Its length to the southwest, stretched as far as his eyes could see. Though he had never ventured so far, he knew the western trail led to the Island Flats where the north and south forks of the Holston joined. In the opposite direction, he recognized the well-worn path that had brought him here and would lead him back to civilization.

Civilization.

The word both lifted his spirits and weighed heavy on his heart. There was so much there for him, but was it truly what he wanted? This land had hooked him as deftly as he had that bluegill the night before. He felt its tug so strongly that it seemed he ought to lean forward to keep from tumbling onto his back.

Back there…

He turned and took a last look back across the Holston. He breathed a deep, satisfying breath, drawing in the memories he would carry in his heart until he returned. For someday he would return, and make this land his home.

Chapter 2

October, 1763

"What do you mean you want to leave?"Old John Wood's booming voice rang out like a cannon. "You have a fine position, our family has standing, and you want to forsake it all to become a dirt farmer?" He spat the last two words as if the very dirt of which he spoke now soiled his mouth. Even seated, his was an intimidating presence. His graying temples did not make him seem old, but rather lent him an air of wisdom and experience. "What kind of foolishness is this? You have been raised better than this."

"It is the most remarkable place I have ever been. You should see it, Father," Jonathan said. Despite his fatigue from the lengthy trek home, the mere thought of that abundant land filled him with vigor. "It is the richest land you could imagine. The streams so choked with fish you can walk across them and never get your boots wet. One time I dropped my rifle. It went off and brought down three deer, a turkey and a slow Injun."

"Your japes will do you no good when those Injuns come calling." John's face remained stolid. "Fool boy. I don't understand all of this. Why would you leave a fine home to cross the mountains, where you most likely are going to up and get yourself killed?"

"It will be fine, Father. I met a Cherokee while I was there. He seemed… civilized." He felt more than a touch condescending describing Duwalla as such, but it was the best description of which he could think at the moment.

"Huh! I suppose that is more than can be said for many of the white men I know." John sat back, folded his hands across his stomach, gone soft in his middle years, and met his son with a level stare, his blue-gray eyes like the sea before a storm. "And what about the Davidson girl?"

"What do you mean?" Jonathan stammered, looking down at the floor, its dark wood polished to a sheen. His stomach was heavy and his throat tight. He just hoped he would not blush in front of his father.

"I might be old, but I am not senile just yet." Now John did laugh. "If you like the mountain country so much, why did you linger on the New River for a week?"

How did his father know? It did not matter. In truth, there was nothing between him and the girl… yet. Nothing but his own hopes. Hopes he thought he had kept reasonably well hidden.

"I thought… I thought to ask her brother for his leave to …"

"You want to ask for her hand?" John said, sympathy painted across his face. "You understand it is not a fit match for you. She is older and… and you are too young!"

"But we're near the same age!" Jonathan protested. "Begging your pardon, Father, but how can that matter in any case?"

John rose from his chair and placed a hand on his son's shoulder. "I am certain it is not easy for you to understand." He sighed. "I liked Samuel Davidson, truly I did. His brother even married into the family back in Albemarle. All of the Davidsons are good men. Did you ever hear how your old Grand-poppy brought himself and the family out of Ulster during the fighting? He helped Sam get set up here, and James should have stayed here too." He shook his head, his eyes taking on a faraway cast. "James married too soon and he has nothing to fall back on. Now he finds himself way down in the New River fighting over a faulty survey. And to top it all off, he took in Nancy as well."

"I *was* surprised to find her down there," Jonathan admitted. "I thought she might…" It was not that he had expected her to wait for him. There was no understanding between them as yet, but he had not expected her to be gone. Fortunately, he had been able to spend time with her down in the New River.

"Just never you mind that." John pressed his fingers to his lined forehead. "Do you not see, she is past eighteen and Sam made no match for her here? She was a liability to Sam and now she's a burden to James. But maidens on the New River are dear, and James will most likely see her betrothed before Christmas.

"It is not that way for you, Jonathan. Not being eldest, you cannot inherit, but you have good prospects. Dr. Walker thinks highly of you or he would not have helped you become a Loyal Land Company surveyor at eighteen years. I would school you to patience, my son. Your situation will improve with time, and I shall find you a suitable match in a few years, once you are established."

Jonathan shook his head. How to make his father understand? It was not that he grieved for lack of opportunities, or envied his brother's position. The life his father had chosen no longer appealed to him. The Northern Neck of Virginia was crowded. Land patents, grants and claims overlapped. Men spent more time in the courts than in their fields. Jonathan craved open spaces, ground on which no white foot had trod. He wanted something different. He felt an affinity for the wilderness, and he knew he would never resist its call.

He suspected that Nancy felt the same way. They had often walked along the South Branch of the Potomac, with James and his wife Catherine as escorts. Nancy loved the low rolling hills of the Northern Neck, but she often spoke about the mystery of the land beyond the Blue Mountains.

And Father was wrong about old Sam Davidson wanting to be shed of her. She had gone to the New River with James and Catherine because she loved James as much as she had loved her father. He had taken her in when their father passed and she was not a burden, because she helped with her three nephews. However, Jonathan knew she also felt the stirring to see what lay beyond those mountains and hoped it would be an adventure they would someday share.

"Father, I understand how successful you have been. The land, the corn rights, bounty from Lord Fairfax for sponsoring immigrants. But don't you remember? You left a similar life of privilege at the Nominy in order to come here and be your own man." The Wood family had settled along the Nominy River in eastern Virginia, enjoying the wealth of the planter's life, yet John had left that behind. "You must have felt something of what I feel. Can you not understand?"

John walked past his son and out onto the front porch where he stood, arms folded across his chest. Jonathan followed him, not breaking the rare silence in which his father contemplated their words.

He looked out across the vast fields, now empty after autumn harvest. Near one of the outbuildings, two slave women minded a large black kettle suspended over an open fire. They sang a low, mournful song as they worked. He did not understand the words, but the haunting melody sent chills down his spine.

The scent of apples mixed with wood smoke drifted through the cool autumn air. *Apple butter*, he thought, and his mouth watered.

He remembered the first time Nancy had let him try some of her apple butter. It had been terrible and he had tried to hide his opinion of it, but something in his face must have given it away. She stormed off, pouting outrageously, and did not come around for nearly a week. He grinned at the memory.

"You are proud of yourself, eh?" John's voice interrupted his thoughts. "You have trapped me, sure as a rabbit in a snare." He clapped his hand on Jonathan's shoulder. "All right, boy. I suppose I do understand, at that. I don't know what might come of it, but go with my blessing."

Chapter 3

October, 1764

Nancy was hauling up a bucket from the creek when Solomon rode up to the fort. She acknowledged his presence in silence by an almost imperceptible bow of her head. Although a stranger to her, he was expected. Solomon's father, and others along the New River, had built Osborne's Fort. Nancy was simply following the conventions of the time, for Solomon was the son of the most influential man in the community.

"Let me do that," he said, taking the bucket from her. Solomon was stout, muscles solid from his life spent clearing land and making long treks in pursuit of game. She took notice of the ease with which he handled the heavy bucket. His movement was unexpected and such contact between an unmarried man and woman made her uneasy.

"Sir, do you not think that I can do for myself?" Her words were only half questioning, the other an assertion of her own standing. Even on the frontier, social conventions were observed and Nancy Davidson was not one to abide such a degree of familiarity with a man not properly introduced. Solomon handed her the bucket awkwardly, having recognized his error.

"I... meant no disrespect. Truly I... Have a good day." He made a quick bow and stepped back from her.

Nancy failed to control her own theft of a momentary glance at Solomon as she turned to walk away. Now, unseen, the corner of her mouth rose in a smirk that emphasized the dimples in her cheeks. She was pleased to have set a boundary that respected tradition. This young man seemed as full of himself as he was full of the vigor of living on the very fringe of civilization in Virginia.

Solomon would soon find that Nancy Davidson had no shortage of suitors. Of course, that was explained by the simple fact that there were few marriageable women on the New River. That, however, belied the reality that Nancy was full of life, the love for life and seemed to find a way to express her every emotion with an economy of grace. Any joy in her childhood in Ulster was tempered with an expectation of religious piety and a rigid code of social conduct. Her arrival in this new community marked the commencement of a spiritual journey as well. One would be hard pressed to say whether Nancy's spirited ways, or her poise accounted for the regard afforded her here on Bridle Creek.

She laughed inwardly as Solomon hurried away. It amused her to see the strong, confident long hunter cowed so easily. He was a good soul, and handsome as well. She was embarrassed that his attention made her feel… desirable. She pushed that vain thought out of her mind. She had work to do.

Jonathan did not know who the young man was to whom Nancy was speaking, but he recognized the smitten look on the young man's face. Jealousy raged inside of him. What had he expected? He saw so little of her, and she was surrounded by potential suitors. Of course she would catch the eye of many men. He would have to do something to change that situation, and right soon.

"Nancy?" he called out to her. She almost dropped her bucket, so startled was she by his sudden appearance.

"Jonathan?" she said, staring at him as if he were an apparition. "What are you doing here? I did not expect you."

"I came to see you," he said, swinging down from the saddle and guiding his horse over to where she waited for him. "Who was that man you were talking to?" he asked, easing the bucket from her slackening grip.

"Oh, just someone from the settlement. He is no one special." Her reddening cheeks told a different story.

"He was acting very familiar for someone who is a 'no one'."

"Why are you so concerned? Do you mean to tell me you aren't romancing Indian princesses when you go off on your trips over the mountains?" She smiled at him.

"No! I never…" Jonathan was suddenly so flustered he could not utter a coherent thought. "I would not…"

"Be still," she said, laying a gentle hand on his shoulder. "I only jest. Honestly! You do let the smallest things upset you." She took the bucket from him and headed toward the family cabin.

Jonathan fell silent. Truth told, it was only around Nancy that such things happened. He was comfortable in any group of people. He could always be counted on to keep the conversation lively with a jape or story, or to help mend a quarrel between friends. Nevertheless, around Nancy he grew nervous and found himself tongue-tied more often than not. Of course, he could not tell her that without looking even more the fool.

"Nancy," he said, falling in step alongside her. "Would you like to hear about my last surveying trip?"

"Did I ask you about your trip?" she asked, then smiled and winked. This time he realized she was joking before he opened his mouth and said something else foolish. "Did you meet any wild Injuns?"

"Yes I did, actually," he said. She raised her eyebrows in surprise, which heartened him. "Duwalla was his name. He was not truly wild, I do not suppose. He spoke English and everything."

"Oh." Nancy sounded disappointed. "Did you kill any bears? I hear tell that some of the long hunters kill bears bigger than them."

"No bear," he said. "I killed a deer, though. A right nice one."

"That is nice," she said, but her tone of voice said it was anything but. She looked up at the darkening sky. "The days are getting shorter," she said. "Winter will be upon us soon. I suppose you will be home until the spring?"

"I will," he replied. His heart pounded and he felt a numb detachment from his surroundings as he realized she had turned the conversation in exactly the direction he had hoped. He would probably make a botch of it but he had to say something before he lost his nerve.

"Nancy, I want to ask you…"

"Jonathan!" A voice boomed. "I'd not heard you were here!" James Davidson, Nancy's brother, appeared from behind the family's cabin, an axe on his shoulder. "And why are you making my sister carry the water? Have you spent so much time in the wilds that you have forgotten how a gentleman treats a lady?"

Jonathan again found himself dumbstruck as Nancy handed him the bucket and stood with her hands on her hips, looking positively affronted. Suddenly she broke into laughter, as did James.

"You know I only jest," James said, clapping Jonathan on the back so hard that some of the water sloshed onto the ground. "It is good to see you. Come inside." He laid a strong hand on Jonathan's shoulder and guided him through the door.

A cheery blaze crackled in the fireplace, holding back the cool autumn breezes that crept through the mud-chinked cabin walls. A hearty stew bubbled in a pot over the fire, filling the room with a mouth-watering aroma. The dirt floor was swept clean, and a home-made quilt adorned the far wall. An oil lamp burned on the trestle table in the center of the room. James offered him a seat on one of the benches that lined the table, and then sat down opposite him. James's wife Catherine appeared just then, and was pleased to see their visitor. She bade Jonathan welcome, and then went about her work.

"Tell me," James said, his brown eyes boring into Jonathan, "how did you find the Tidewater when you were last there?"

"Well, I rode north, and there it was," Jonathan said. They shared a laugh, and Jonathan related the latest news to James, Catherine, and Nancy.

"Tell me about the land out west," James said. "You might have heard that we've been having problems with some of our claims in these parts. I might have to contemplate another move. What is it like out there?"

"It is the most beautiful land I have ever seen," Jonathan said. "Open land for farming. Forests filled with game, cold, clear streams with the biggest fish you can imagine." Nancy, who was stirring the stew, paused to listen, and Jonathan warmed to his task. "You should see the mountains in the morning. It's like the scripture says: God touched the mountain and it smoked."

"So it is true what they say?" Nancy whispered. "The mountains do smoke?"

"A sure as I am sitting here," Jonathan averred, pleased to have finally gotten her attention. "I have never seen anything like it."

"What I want to know," James said, "is can you spit off your front porch without hitting your neighbor's barn? I don't like any place that is too crowded. I like my neighbors, but only at a distance, mind you."

"There is plenty of room," Jonathan said. "The land is there for the taking if you are willing to work it. But you can't wait. The companies are already taking up the best land."

James folded his arms across his chest and leaned back, staring at the fire in the hearth. "You've given me much to think about. That you have. And what about you? Are you so taken with this land that you might settle on it yourself? A man your age should probably be thinking about a home and a family, should he not?"

"I think I might like to settle there," Jonathan said. "My father would prefer that I continue surveying, but I have other ideas. I'll be headed to Williamsburg to file my patents for the year, and then I need to begin making some definite plans for the future." He tried to meet Nancy's eye, but she turned back to her cooking.

He realized that now was not the time to speak of an arrangement between the two of them. What had he to offer? He lived his life in the saddle, rarely setting foot in civilization, and then only for a short while. Until he could offer her something solid, a place to call home, he could not ask for her hand. His dreams of living over the mountains were only that. Dreams could not feed a wife and children. It was time for him to make something more of himself.

His visit lasted only a bit longer. James had work to do, as did Catherine and Nancy. He would have dearly loved to go for a walk with Nancy, but her brother did not have time to escort them. They said their goodbyes, with Jonathan promising to return in the spring. He rode away, determined that when he next saw her, he would be a man worthy of her love.

Chapter 4

December, 1764

Jonathan drew his cloak tight to his chest as a chill wind blew through Williamsburg. He stepped out onto Duke of Gloucester Street, dodging the bustle of traffic that flowed through the capitol city. Walking toward the capitol building, he shivered with excitement. There was something about this city that made him feel… vibrant… alive, as if the very pulse of Virginia beat here.

A visit to Williamsburg was always an exciting diversion, and he always felt a great sense of completion upon registering his patents for the year. He would find a meal and a drink, and then off to bed for the night before beginning his journey back to the New River to spend Christmas with Nancy and her family. He had thought of little else since leaving her. Deep inside, he still struggled with the abiding fear that he was not yet good enough for her. He needed to make a stake in the world. He needed something to call his own.

Wrapped in his thoughts, he give little notice to those milling about him.

"Jonathan Wood!" A voice called out from the bustle of foot traffic along the thoroughfare.

Jonathan stopped in the middle of the road, barely avoiding being run down by a man on horseback. The rider scowled at him as he trotted past.

"Over here!" A fair-skinned young man with brown hair was waving his cap above the milling throng.

"Isaac?" Jonathan could not hide his surprise.

Isaac Burwell was his cousin on his mother's side. His was a family of planters from Northumberland County on the bay. His Cavalier-style clothing underscored his family's affluence.

"What are you doing here?" Jonathan asked.

"I'm reading the law," Isaac said, with a touch of self-importance. "How have you been? The last time I saw you was at cousin Emily's wedding. Now that was a fine time."

Jonathan remembered the wedding all too well. Rather, he remembered the night of carousing with Isaac after the wedding, and the painful aftermath of their intemperance.

"We must take some time to catch up. Perhaps a cup of coffee at Charlton's? Better yet, let me stand you to a drink in Shield's Tavern," Isaac said, taking him by the arm and turning him around.

"But while we are inside, please do not let on that you are a borderman. I do have a reputation to uphold." The crinkles at the corners of his eyes belied his seriousness.

"Perhaps after we have our drink, I'll buy you a dress," Jonathan retorted. "It would go well with those lovely curls."

Laughing, Isaac swept off his plumed hat and bowed as he opened the door for his cousin. A blue haze of smoke and sound enveloped Jonathan as he stepped inside. There was an air of urgency about the place, as if serious business lay beneath each boisterous laugh and overloud conversation.

Jonathan found a seat at an out-of-the way table in the corner and sat taking in the scene. Well-dressed men crowded around tables and bustled past one another, most careful not to spill their ale, coffee, or claret. Snatches of conversation drifted through the din. Two men at the table closest to him were talking in high, nasal voices about the Sugar Act, which had impacted the northern colonies to a much greater degree than those in the south. The rich aroma of pipe smoke wafted through the air, putting him to mind of evenings spent as a child, sitting at his father's knee by the fireplace, listening to fascinating stories of his Scottish ancestors.

Isaac returned with two foaming tankards of ale and slid onto the trestle bench across from Jonathan.

"So, how goes the wilderness?" His voice lacked the condescension that Jonathan expected from his wealthy cousin. "Still wild, I imagine?"

"Not so much," Jonathan said, sipping his ale. It had a strong, rich flavor. Isaac would, no doubt, have bought the best. "I rather prefer it to civilization and its massed throngs."

"Is it as dangerous as they say?"

"I don't know the 'they' of whom you are speaking," Jonathan replied, "but I've been safe so far."

"Good to know," Isaac muttered. His eyes were on his ale, which sat untouched on the table. He was clearly distracted, but by what, Jonathan had no idea. "Is there a girl?" Isaac was suddenly cheery again.

"A girl?"

"I can tell from the look in your eyes." Isaac smiled and leaned toward Jonathan, lowering his voice in conspiratorial fashion. "Who is she? Not some wild woman from the backwoods, I hope."

"Hardly." Jonathan chuckled and took another drink, taking pleasure in making Isaac wait. "Her name is Nancy. There is no understanding between us as yet, but I believe she is amenable."

"Amenable. How romantic you are, cousin." Isaac's sardonic comment cut through the din in the room, causing Jonathan to flush. "What is stopping you? Your father? Money?" He must have seen something in Jonathan's expression, because he locked on like a hound after the fox. "That is it, isn't it? Oh, don't look at me like that, Jonathan. I know you well enough to understand that you are too stubborn and prideful to accept even what help your father might give to a son who is not eldest. I also know that surveying, though an admirable trade, will not make you wealthy." He slipped his hand beneath his cloak and drew forth a folded square of aged paper. "Which is why it is providential that we should meet at this time and place."

"What is that?" Jonathan did not mean to snap at Isaac, but his cousin's ability to pierce the very heart of the matter annoyed him.

"This is the key to our fortunes." He waited for Jonathan to ask for a further explanation, but he was in no mood for Isaac's flair for the dramatic. "This, my dear kinsman…"He unfolded the paper and lay it out on the table between them. "…is a map to Swift's lost silver mine."

Jonathan groaned and rolled his eyes. "What are you thinking? It's a myth."

"Not according to the man who gave me these directions. He has been there."

"He probably saw your hat and took you for a fool. You'll be wearing a tri-cornered before long."

Isaac ignored the jest. "I could see the truth in his eyes."His voice lowered into an urgent whisper. "He is telling the truth. Jonathan, think of the money we could make. You could set yourself up, you and your young lady would not have to live…"He waved his hand, unable to complete the thought. 'Poor' was likely the word he had in mind, but he would not want to offend Jonathan—not when he needed Jonathan's help. And, in fairness, Isaac was sometimes thoughtless, but not heartless.

"Even if he is telling the truth, it is not our mine. It belongs to Swift, if he even exists."

"It is not Swift's mine, nor does it belong to anyone else…"Isaac paused as a serious-looking man with a prominent forehead and overlong nose passed by, arguing loudly with a short, thick man with a florid face and bulging eyes. Jonathan caught the words "Bacon" and "treason." He assumed Bacon referred to a man and not the meat. Bacon had disagreed with his stomach from time to time, but he would not go so far as to refer to indigestion as "treason."

"Mr. Henry," Isaac called, half-rising. "It is good to see you again, Sir."

If the man was annoyed by the interruption, he did not let it show. His brow furrowed for a half-second, then he smiled.

"Burwell. A pleasure to see you. No need to stand on my account. How is your family?" Even in polite conversation, Henry's eyes shone with the intensity of an eagle.

"They are well sir, and yours?"

"As well as can be expected in times such as these." He arched an eyebrow at Isaac, as if a struck by a sudden thought. "You are reading for Bartholomew Dandridge, are you not?"

"Yes I am," Isaac said, obviously pleased that Henry knew something of him. "I had spoken with George Wythe, but he has already taken on someone."

"Ah! Young Thomas Jefferson," Henry said, smiling. "He is an opinionated young fellow, is he not?

"That he is," Isaac said, lowering his gaze. He apparently did not care for this Jefferson fellow. "Forgive me, but I feel he permits too many liberties to… certain sorts."

Henry obviously was not interested in continuing in this vein of conversation. "Does Dandridge still keep offices on Custis Square?"

"He does," Isaac replied.

"Very good. I need to speak with him. Perhaps I shall see you there. I must be off." He nodded to

Jonathan and strode away. Polite, but not enough so as to invite further conversation.

"Patrick Henry." The corners of Isaac's mouth curled ever so slightly downward. "An important man. I do not necessarily agree with his politics, but I admire his zeal."He shook his head as if seeing Henry had cast a fog on his mind that he was now trying to clear.

"As I was saying, the mine belongs to no one. It is in Indian territory, beyond the line set down by the proclamation."

Jonathan grimaced. Issued in 1863, the proclamation to which his cousin referred had driven many settlers back off of their claims, though others chose to defy the treaty between the Cherokee and the royal governor. In any case, the new line making the westernmost limit of settlement had not made things any easier for him as a surveyor. It did not matter. People would continue pressing on westward.

"So the mine belongs to the Indians," he said, knowing the folly of his words but not wanting to give in to Isaac.

"How many Indians do you see carrying a pick and shovel? Really, now. The silver is there for the taking!"

"But it is winter…"

"Virginia winter!" Isaac's voice took on a wheedling tone. "It is not as if we were in

Massachusetts or… Canada." Whether Isaac did not know the names of any colonies north of Massachusetts, or simply did not care, Jonathan could not say. "Besides, that is the very reason we should go now. Others would not try it in the wintertime."

"Others are apparently wiser than you. Have you ever slept outside in the winter? No matter how hard you try, you can never get warm all the way through. The wind bites through your clothing, and your nose always feels as if it's going to fall off. It's dangerous as well."

"Bah!" Isaac waved the question away. "You will take care of us. I know politics and money. You know the mountains. I have no reservations about placing my life in your capable hands."

Isaac was manipulating him, just like he always had, but the compliment did make Jonathan swell a touch.

"Let us try it. If we do not find the mine, you have lost only a few weeks. But if we are successful…"He spread his hands apart and looked Jonathan in the eye, letting Jonathan's imagination complete the picture.

He made a compelling argument. Jonathan was skeptical, but the idea of a treasure hunt intrigued him. And Isaac was right; if the tale was true… He could not entertain that possibility. It was too much to hope for.

Then again, if he could make his next visit to the New River as a wealthy man, how much more amenable would James Davidson be to a match between him and Nancy? It was foolishness. He was a simple surveyor, not an adventurer.

Then he remembered the way Nancy had looked at the young man Jonathan had seen her talking with on his last visit. He recalled her tone of voice as she spoke almost dreamily about long hunters bringing down bears. Why could he not have an adventure? He was as good a man as any.

He took a deep breath and let it out slowly. He could not believe he was about to agree to this, but the temptation was too great.

"All right, Isaac." He put his ale aside and sat up a bit straighter. "Let me take a closer look at your map."

Chapter 5

January, 1765

"That looks like the peak he describes." Jonathan took a second look at the map, and squinted against the bitter winter wind as he gazed up at the distinctive rock formation.

"I was right, wasn't I?" Isaac was almost childlike in his glee. His complaints had been surprisingly few during their trek into the mountains, though the weather and Isaac's inexperience had slowed their progress. Christmas had come and gone, celebrated with a bottle of rum shared beneath a lean-to shelter in front of a crackling fire.

"Not much farther now. Can you believe it? We are going to be rich men!" Isaac clapped Jonathan on the shoulder.

"That depends on what waits for us at the top of that mountain." Jonathan returned the map to his oilcloth pack and urged his horse forward.

The way soon grew too steep for riding. They dismounted and led their horses as far up the slope as they dared. Finally, they could take the creatures no further.

"I can see the stone formation from here. You wait here with the horses. It should not take me too long to make the climb," Jonathan instructed.

"But I want to come with you!"Isaac argued. "The mine…"

"We do not know for certain if the mine is there or not. Wait here with the horses. I'll be back in a thrice."

Isaac's countenance darkened, but he said nothing. He snatched the reins of Jonathan's horse and stood gazing up at the mountaintop.

The frozen crust of dirt and leaves crunched underfoot as Jonathan made his climb. Twice he lost his footing on frozen stone hidden under a thin veneer of pine needles and fell heavily onto his hands and knees. The last twenty feet of the climb he made on all fours, clinging to tree roots and stone outcroppings to pull himself up.

He reached the top of the mountain and paused to take in the scene below. Even in the dead of winter, with bare trees reaching skeletal hands up to grasp the blanket of gray sky, it was a sight to behold. A silver ribbon of river wound through scattered clusters of evergreen. He inhaled the icy air, as if breathing in life itself.

According to the directions, the entrance to the mine lay somewhere near this stone bluff.

"About the width of a hogshead," Jonathan recited, scanning the open space, "dropping down ten feet, and then leveling off."

A large boulder immediately caught his eye. It was broad enough to cover an opening the width of a hogshead, and it stood out of place on the otherwise smooth, stone surface. He ran his fingers over it. There was neither lichen nor moss growing there, and it was of a lighter shade than the native rock. If someone had gone to the trouble of hauling it all the way up here, they must have had good reason.

He stepped back and scrutinized the boulder, looking for the best way to unseat it. It was roughly spherical, and it appeared that the bottom was set in a hole or recess. Figuring he had nothing to lose, he bent his knees, grabbed hold of two imperfections in the stone, and heaved.

It rocked, but fell back again. Another heave. It rocked a little farther, enough for him to see a hole beneath. His heart raced. He could call Isaac to help him, but he did not like the idea of leaving the horses untended. Granted, their encounters with people of any kind had been limited to a few distant sightings of Cherokee and Mingo, but he did not want to take the chance.

After a quick search, he found a sturdy limb as long and thick as his forearm. Laying it down next to the stone, he rocked the stone forward again and used his foot to work the limb into the opening. Now he was able to reset his feet and put all his strength into the lift. His calves and thighs burned, and he grunted with the effort, but finally he succeeded in rolling the stone out of its resting place and into a clump of juniper. He stumbled forward and nearly fell down into the hole, but caught himself just in time.

He knelt and peered into the darkness. It was not deep — perhaps half again as tall as he. Cracks in the rock, and two loose stones at the bottom, afforded steps and handholds, assuring he would not find himself in a trap from which he could not escape. The pungent smell that indicated a predator's lair was absent. Feeling cautiously optimistic, he made his way down.

At the bottom, the passageway cut a horizontal shaft back into the mountain. He lit a taper and crawled forward, letting its faint light show the way. The way narrowed as he moved deeper, the walls seeming to close in around him. When he had crawled perhaps thirty feet, the tunnel ended in a solid wall of rock.

Disappointment pinched the back of his throat and he gritted his teeth. It had all been for nothing. He and Isaac had been fools to believe in the legend, and now they had wasted weeks. Weeks when he could have been sitting in front of a warm fire, or paying court to Nancy. Now he would ride into the New River months late, with no explanation that would not make him look a complete fool.

The circle of faint light fell upon something wedged into a crack in the wall. He carefully worked it loose, and held it out in front of him, moving the light closer so he could see. It was a shell gorget the size of his palm and inlaid with an intricate design. It hung from a rawhide thong. Unable to make out any details in the near-dark, he slipped the rawhide around his neck and tucked the gorget beneath his coat before backing out of the tunnel.

He clambered out into open air, already debating how to break it to Isaac that they had failed. He stepped out onto the stone bluff, breathing deeply of the clear, mountain air. He closed his eyes, but opened them again almost immediately. Something was not right.

Winter in the wilderness was quiet, but just now it was abnormally so. There was a feeling of tension in the air. His rifle was back with Isaac and the horses, but he had his tomahawk. He found comfort in the smooth, solid handle as he drew it from his belt. It was perfectly weighted for throwing, and he was better than most.

Quietly slipping into a nearby cluster of fir, he scanned the surrounding woods. He could see Isaac far down the slope, still standing with the horses. He was not alone.

Isaac had not yet noticed the men who were creeping up on him from all sides. Two of them, at least, were armed with hunting rifles. He gritted his teeth and began to make a plan. If he...

"Lay it on the ground." The voice was filled with youthful urgency, and hinted at a touch of fear. That was not good. A frightened person made bad decisions. Jonathan set the tomahawk on the ground, careful to move slowly so as not to startle the fellow into doing something foolish.

"Git on over there with yer friend."

Jonathan took his time, painfully aware of the weapon trained on his back. The two men who had been creeping up on Isaac now made their presence known and were guarding him closely. Isaac's eyes, burning with indignation, met Jonathan's, and Jonathan feared for a moment that his cousin would try something foolish. Thankfully, he remained still.

"What did ye' find in there?" One of the men who watched Isaac spoke up. He kept his rifle trained on Jonathan's cousin, but inclined his head toward the cave. As he turned his head, the sun glinted off his aquiline nose and olive skin.

"Nothing," Jonathan replied. "Only an empty cave." Isaac frowned at him, but Jonathan ignored him. "You can see I am not carrying anything."

"What were ye' doing in there, anyhow?" His voice carried no hint of suspicion, but merely curiosity.

"The silver mine." The youth who was guarding Jonathan stepped into view. He was short and solidly built. There was a trace of Indian in his features, but his thick lips and wavy, auburn hair spoke of mixed ancestry. He was no more than fifteen years old. "Every time one of y'uns gets lost up here, it's because of the silver mine. Well, there ain't no silver mine." The veins in his neck and forehead bulged, emphasizing the tension that was evident in his voice and posture.

"We have come to the same conclusion." Jonathan kept his voice calm and his manner easy. "If you will be so kind as to return my tomahawk, you will have no more trouble from us. I give you my word."

The three young men exchanged uncertain glances.

"Let's just let 'em go, Elvas." The young man who had first spoken to Isaac stepped back and lowered his rifle. "They don't have nothin' and they ain't hurtin' nobody."

The third youth, darker of skin than the other two, with glossy indigo hair, finally spoke up. "Take 'em to Mr. Cumbow. Let him decide."

Elvas thought for a moment, his face twisted into a grimace. Finally, he nodded. "Y'uns lead your horses. Don't try nothin' crazy. Jist follow Harlan. Matthew and me will be behind you."

They set off behind the dark-skinned youth, who led them on a winding path through thick stands of pine. The need for stealth now absent, they set a quick pace, frozen leaves crunching underfoot, ringing out like gunshots in the midst of the still winter's day.

"You did find something," Isaac whispered. "It was not truly empty?"

"No talkin' up there." Elvas tried to sound authoritative, but failed miserably.

Jonathan looked at his cousin and shook his head, trying to convey with his eyes that there was nothing to talk about. In fact, they had failed miserably. There had been no silver mine, only a dead end.

Isaac flushed, and his eyes flared. He clearly did not believe Jonathan. He kept his silence, though, as they had been instructed.

Elvas and Matthew, for their part, did not follow Elvas's injunction. The two of them kept up a hushed conversation as they made their way through the frozen forest.

"You can't take them back to the village," Matthew pleaded. "They ain't like us."

"We have to. I done decided." Elvas's voice held little emotion.

"But then they'll know where we live. They kin bring others back. You know what happens when Tidewater folk comes around..."

"I know just what happens, and I'm tired of it!" Elvas snapped. "Besides, they done know we live here now. If they took a mind to come back here and find us, there wouldn't be no stoppin' 'em. That's why we got to take 'em to Cumbow. Now you jest hush yer mouth!"

Jonathan had no idea what happened when men from the Tidewater came to these parts. In fact, he was surprised that any had done so. If Isaac knew, he gave no sign.

The continued to trudge along, wondering what lay ahead.

Chapter 6

They arrived in a settlement like none Jonathan had ever seen. A large cabin, actually two cabins joined by a dogtrot, stood at the center of the small village. Other structures varied in size and completeness; some were simple log cabins with mud fireplaces, while others were little more than lean-tos. Several lean goats and a few undersized cattle were held in a split rail pen on the far end of the village.

As their captors led them hastily through the settlement, an eerie silence fell among the villagers, who eyed them through dark, suspicious eyes. Even the children fell silent and drew away from the two newcomers. A man with skin so dark it was almost blue espied them and disappeared behind a nearby half-cabin. He was probably a runaway slave, not that Jonathan cared one whit.

When they arrived at the door of the big cabin, Elvas moved to the front, swallowed hard, and knocked. They waited, only the clucking of guinea fowl disturbing the silence.

Finally, the door scraped open and a dark, angular man of late middle years stepped out. Silver sprinkled his black hair and thick eyebrows. Though he was merely of average height, his posture and bearing made it seem as if he was looking down at the group. His eyes passed over both Jonathan and Isaac with barely a hint of interest, and fell upon Elvas.

"Mister Cumbow, um..." His face reddening, Elvas hung his head and scuffed his foot on the hard-packed dirt. "I ah... that is to say we... we brung these men to you."

Cumbow's face remained impassive as he stared at the young man, who still would not meet his eye. Finally, he turned to Jonathan.

"Please come inside." He stood aside for Jonathan and Isaac to enter. "Not you three," he said to the youths who had brought Jonathan and Isaac to the settlement. "I shall speak with you outside."

The young men all looked as if they had swallowed chewing tobacco. Elvas gulped and nodded.

"I beg your pardon," Cumbow said to Jonathan. "Please have a seat." He nodded to them and closed the door behind him.

The house was simple and the furnishings plain. A few finely worked pieces of silver lined a rough-hewn mantle above the fireplace.

"I remember you." A familiar voice startled him. He turned to see a tall Indian leaning against the wall by the fireplace.

"Duwalla? Is it really you?" He had not forgotten his first meeting with the Cherokee. He and Duwalla clasped hands like old friends. He introduced Isaac, who merely nodded and did not offer his hand.

Duwalla ignored the rebuff and turned to Jonathan. "What are you doing here, Jonathan Wood?"

Don't tell him," Isaac snapped. "Where we go and what we do is our business."

Duwalla eyed Isaac with a curious expression and then turned up his head and laughed. "Duwalla did not take Jonathan Wood for a treasure hunter. I am surprised. Tell me, did my friend find the silver mine?"

"No, we did not." Jonathan saw no point in lying, and it was unlikely he could feel any more embarrassed than he already did, having been led into town under the guard of three fuzzy-cheeked boys. "We had a map, but it only led to an empty cave."

"I shall be wanting my map back," Isaac said, his hands folded across his chest. "I did not get to see this cave for myself."

"Take it." Jonathan shrugged. "It is in the oilcloth bag tied to my saddle." The weight of the folly he and Isaac had undertaken was now settling firmly onto his shoulders. He wanted to sink down to the floor and not get up again. How foolish he had been.

"Perhaps there is no mine," Duwalla said without elaboration.

"No? Then where does all this silver come from?" Isaac gestured at the various items of silver on the mantle.

"The people who live here, they make them." Duwalla said. "They melt down old things made of silver. I do not know for certain. I spend little time here."

"I can see why." Isaac scowled, looking for all the world like he had bitten into a crabapple. "Their hospitality leaves much to be desired." He brushed at the sleeves of his coat as if he could wipe away the very thought of this place.

"You are a *Tidewater* man," Duwalla spoke the word with obvious distaste. "They do not trust your kind. Tidewater men come through this place and say they are hunting foxes, but they are hunting women. If one of their women is not old or heavy with child, she must hide or else..." His meaning was clear.

"A Tidewater gentleman would never lay with the likes of these." Despite his protestations, Isaac's voice held little conviction, and he met neither Duwalla's nor Jonathan's eye.

"Why don't they fight?" Jonathan had no reason to love these people, but what Duwalla described was barbaric.

"They wish to be left alone. If they fight, maybe the Tidewater men come back with more guns, and it is worse the next time. The village moves. That is why you do not see many cabins."

A shrill scream broke the quiet of the village, followed by the clattering of hooves and shouts of raucous glee. Jonathan sprang to the door and flung it open. Two men, dressed in fine hunting clothes that were clearly worse for the wear, came galloping into the village. The man in the lead, a pale young man with a windburned face, fired his flintlock pistol in the air, laughing maniacally. The second man held a shrieking girl across his saddle.

"You can see I tell the truth," Duwalla said, a note of sadness in his voice.

Jonathan reacted without thinking. Elvas was standing dumbstruck nearby. Jonathan slipped his tomahawk out of Elvas's belt and dashed into the street.

The lead rider looked down in surprise, and then pointed his pistol at Jonathan, forgetting he had already fired it. Jonathan grabbed a handful of coat and yanked the rider from his saddle. The man fell hard to the ground, landing on his side, and his pistol slipping from his grasp. Jonathan picked up the pistol and flung it at the second rider, a broad-shouldered fellow with a long chin, who was struggling to both hold on to the squirming girl and bring his own weapon to bear. He flinched away from Jonathan's throw, which bought a precious second.

Jonathan hurled his tomahawk, aiming for the man's gun hand. His aim was off just a bit, and the weapon bit deep into the man's forearm. The man cursed, and his shot went high. Jonathan yanked him down from his horse, bringing the girl tumbling down as well. He tried to catch her, and managed to slow her fall enough that she landed in a rough heap, but not too hard.

The man who had fallen first, struggled to climb to his feet, but Jonathan kicked him in the temple, and he slumped to the ground, his eyes rolling back in his head. The second man knelt in the middle of the road clutching his bleeding arm. He stared at Jonathan, his eyes afire with impotent rage.

"You dare put your hands on Augustine Hobbs, you filthy backwoods..."

"I should not finish that sentence were I in your position."Jonathan reached down and slipped the man's hunting knife out of his belt, then did the same for the other fellow, who was trying to sit up, but obviously wanted no more of this fight. "You might find yourself scalped."

"By these... half-breeds?" Despite his pain, Hobbs managed to sneer.

"By me." Jonathan ran a finger along the edge of his knife. "After all, I am no more than a filthy backwoodsman."

"Jonathan, you cannot do this! These are white men! Englishmen!" Isaac ran into the street and stepped between him and the two men. They stared at one another for a long moment. "I do not know you anymore," Isaac whispered, his face twisted in a scornful sneer.

"And for the very first time, I truly know you." Jonathan met his cousin's gaze with determination and a touch of sadness. "Bind this one's arm, and be gone with the three of you."

Isaac's eyes bulged with shock. "Fine, then, but I want my map."

"The devil take you and your map! It's nothing but foolishness. I have wasted months looking for nothing."

"You say it is nothing." Isaac's voice was too low to carry beyond the two of them. "But how do I know you are not trying to keep it to yourself?"

"Take your map. I told you where it is." Jonathan turned away, moving slowly so as to hold on to his emotions. He retrieved his tomahawk, scraping it in the dirt to clean the worst of the blood, before collecting the men's pistols. The villagers had caught the men's horses, and they brought them to Jonathan, who also took possession of their powder horns.

"What are you doing? Those belonged to us." Hobbs winced as one of the elder women removed his blood-soaked coat and made to clean and dress his wound.

"I'll not have you coming back and making trouble for these people. You may have your knives back when you leave. If you have no provisions, I will give you dried meat for your ride back. You won't starve."

"You are not taking anything of mine." Isaac stood with his arms folded across his chest, clutching his map. "I am leaving with these men and I am taking all of my possessions."

Jonathan was not surprised, but knowing that his ties with Isaac were likely broken beyond repair stung him. "You know very well you could not stop me, Isaac. But I will allow you to take your pistol and powder. Your rifle stays with me. Truly, I do not know why I am bothering. You shoot like a woman anyhow."

Still watching from in front of the big cabin, Elvas snickerd, but suppressed it in a false cough under Cumbow's stern gaze.

After Hobbs's wound was cleaned and bound, he, Isaac, and the third man, whose name was Grimes, were mounted and on their way out of the village under the watchful eyes of Jonathan, Elvas, Matthew, and Harlan. Neither Isaac nor Grimes met Jonathan's eye, but Hobbs turned and stared at him, his blue eyes burning with hate. Jonathan had made an enemy.

When the riders had finally disappeared from sight, the tension seemed to drain from the village, as if everyone had been holding his breath in unison. A short, wiry man with a broad forehead and a hatchet nose approached Jonathan, holding out his hand tentatively, as if he feared Jonathan might bite it. Behind him stood the girl Jonathan had rescued. Though she looked at him shyly, she appeared relatively unshaken by what had just transpired.

"My name is Carrico. This is my daughter, Rachel." Rachel's mother must have been an Indian, for Rachel had the distinctive high cheekbones and sleek, glossy hair. Her brown eyes shone with gratitude. She was young, perhaps fifteen, but the promise of mature beauty was already evident.

Jonathan clasped the man's hand and nodded first to him, and then to Rachel.

"You must go now."

Jonathan turned to find Cumbow standing behind him.

"We shall now have to move our village. You must go." He turned and walked back into his house, leaving Jonathan standing in stunned silence, staring blankly at Cumbow's back. The villagers seemed to take their leader's words as an order to shun the man who had saved one of their own. They all turned and went about their business, speaking not a word to him.

Elvas appeared at his side, leading Jonathan's horse.

"I apologize," he said. "I done the wrong thing. But I thank ye' for..."

"You need not apologize. I understand now why you did it." Jonathan was happy that at least one of the villagers was still speaking to him. He now had a long ride to the New River ahead of him; a ride in which he would have to come up with a plausible, yet not embarrassing, explanation for his absence.

"May I travel with you?" Duwalla rode up beside him, mounted on a lean roan stallion.

"I would like that." The company of someone who knew the woods and did not seem to be a great talker would be a welcome change from his travels with Isaac.

They rode out of the village at a slow trot. Only Rachel looked at them as they rode away, and she raised her hand in a tentative wave. Jonathan smiled as they passed her. She was a pretty thing. The thought of those men bespoiling one so delicate sickened him. He thought he had done a good thing. No... he *knew* he had done a good thing. Why did they treat him as if he were as bad as Hobbs and Grimes?

"I do not understand it," he said. "They act as though I have done them a great evil. They were all standing by and watching it happen. Who else was going to save her?"

"They do not think as you do. The girl would have survived. They only want no more of those." Duwalla nodded to a cluster of low structures that looked like houses in miniatures.

"Are those graves?" He had never seen their like. There was something eerie about them, as if the spirits of the departed abided there still.

Duwalla nodded.

Jonathan looked at the final resting places of those who had gone home to their heavenly reward. Of course no one wanted to die, but a life needed to be worth living, or what was the point of it all?

"Why can't they understand?" He spoke more to himself than to his companion. "Sometimes, you have to fight, even if the battle seems already lost."

Duwalla regarded him with an appraising look, then turned his gaze to the woods that lay ahead. Each man lost in his own thoughts, they rode onin the silence of a bright winter's day.

Chapter 7

March, 1765

The first hints of spring were upon the New River when Jonathan returned. He and Duwalla had parted ways ten miles back. As he rode along, people called his name, some asking where he had been. He acknowledged them all, but did not tarry. He had been away far too long.

There were many unfamiliar faces now, strangers who had arrived in the time since he had last been here, and though this place would seem deserted to someone from Williamsburg, it had already grown uncomfortably crowded to him.

James Davidson was outside when Jonathan arrived at the Davidson homestead. He looked up in surprise when Jonathan called his name, and a smile broke across his face.

"Why, Jonathan Wood! I wondered if we would be seeing you again. We expected you some time ago."

"I know. The delay was regrettable." Jonathan hoped James would not ask too many questions about what had kept him. He would prefer not to admit his folly. "Are you well?"

"I am a mite better now that I know you are alive. Truth be told, we had given you up for dead. We keep hearing rumors of Indian trouble, and feared something had happened to you. I'm thankful to learn we were wrong."

"Thank you. I am thankful to be in one piece. Is Nancy in?"

"Nancy? Oh, well, as to that..."Davidson ran his hand through his hair and looked up at the sky. The set of his jaw and look in his eyes told Jonathan that something was very wrong. Had she taken ill? Had she… "I am sorry to be the one to tell you…" Davidson continued.

"Has something happened to her?"An icy cold grew in the pit of Jonathan's stomach. So many things could go wrong in the settlements: fevers, accidents, snakebite, wounds that festered... He just never believed anything could happen to Nancy. He was almost afraid to ask the question. "Is she all right?"

"Oh, yes, she is fine. I just do not know how to tell you..."

"Jonathan? Is that you?" The voice was like a choir of angels.

"Nancy!" He hopped down from his horse and walked toward her, but stopped when he saw her look of uncertainty.

She halted in mid-stride and took a step backward, paling visibly.

"What is wrong?" He had expected her to be surprised, even angry, but she looked almost frighten.

"I thought you were dead. Everyone said you had to be."

"You can see that I am not, but for the life of me, you do not seem happy about it."

She suddenly stalked up to him and slapped him across the face. The blow stung, but the shock numbed it. What was wrong with her?

"You promised you would come back for Christmas!" she whispered. "I told myself you had simply been delayed. And then I waited and waited, but you never came!" Tears flowed freely down her cheeks.

"I was delayed, and I am sorry about that, but I am here now." He moved closer to her and reached out to take her hand, but she drew away again.

"Jonathan, I am married!"

The icy feeling in the pit of his stomach now spread throughout his body. This was what James Davidson had not wanted to tell him. He looked from Nancy to her brother, then back at Nancy, hoping that this was a poor joke, but their grave expressions told him it was not.

"I will just be right over here if you have need of me," Davidson said. He moved to stand near the house, giving them a modicum of privacy while not leaving them alone together. If it was true, and Nancy was now a married woman, this entire conversation was highly inappropriate.

"You were away for so long," she sobbed. "At first I thought you had forgotten me, or changed your mind about your feelings for me. I was so angry with you. I started talking with Solomon Osborne when he was in from his hunting trips. He told me tales of his hunts, and he helped me not dwell upon how you had abandoned me."

"But I did not." Jonathan's voice was husky with emotion, and his throat felt as though it would swell shut from grief.

"I did not know that," she replied. "Finally, when no one had word of you for so long, everyone just decided you must be dead. And then I felt terrible for having been angry with you, and so upset that I had lost you." Tears welled in her eyes. "Solomon comforted me, helped me through it." She paused, her face a mirror of the grief he felt. "I am so sorry. My feelings for you will never change, but I am Solomon's wife now." She hung her head. "You should know that he is a good man. He treats me kindly."

The world was spinning. One foolish decision and everything had changed. It was all Jonathan could do to remain on his feet. He took a deep breath and forced his lips into something that was almost a tight smile.

"Congratulations on your marriage." His voice was icy cold. "I wish you both well." Unable to say more, he turned and mounted his horse.

"Wait!" Nancy cried. "You don't have to go so soon!"

Jonathan did not answer. He dug his heels into his horse's flanks and set off at a canter. He did not slow his pace until night had fallen and he was well beyond the bounds of the New River.

He had no appetite, despite not having eaten all day. A cool, damp wind whispered through the trees, sending chills through his weary body. He had neither the energy nor the desire to build a fire, but the prospect of a night wrapped in a blanket on the cold ground held no appeal for him. He sighed and looked around for a place to camp. He had excellent night vision, and he spotted a thicket of spruce in which he could find shelter from the wind. He was guiding his horse in that direction when a glint of fire caught his eye.

It was only a glimmer. Whoever had built the fire had hidden it well. He stared at the place where he'd noticed the light, and soon he saw a bit of cinder float into the air, and his nose caught the scent of smoke.

He dismounted and led his horse toward the fire. It was possible, he supposed, that whoever had lit this fire might not welcome visitors, but right now he did not care. Let the fellow shoot him and be done with it.

A tall, angular man sat cross-legged before the fire. He had a strong chin, and a nose that was a touch too large for his face. He was dressed in typical frontier garb: fringed hunting shirt, leggings, moccasins, and a beaver hat. His rifle lay across his lap, but he held a cup in both hands. He looked up at Jonathan with polite interest.

"I reckoned you weren't no Injun, the way you was traipsin' through here. You near scared my rabbits off their skewers." He nodded toward the cookfire, where two rabbits were roasting. The aroma was heavenly.

Jonathan's mouth watered at the smell of roasting meat, and his stomach rumbled. He tied his horse to a nearby tree and stepped into the small ring of firelight.

The man leaned forward and eyed him with a raptor-like gaze. He seemed to take in every detail in an instant.

"Is something ailin' ye?"

"A woman." Jonathan sank to the ground and stretched his feet out in front of him. He was tired and felt like he'd been beaten.

"Now that does explain a thing or two." The fellow chuckled and reached to turn the rabbits. He had shielded his fire from prying eyes in the same way Jonathan always did—enclosing it in a screen of bark. "Am I to take it you don't ordinarily go shambling through the woods like a drunken bull?"

"No." Jonathan grinned in spite of himself. "Not if I can help it." He was suddenly embarrassed at the fact he had barged into this man's campsite without so much as an introduction. "I am Jonathan Wood." He offered his hand.

"Dan'l Boone." Boone's hands were callused and he had a strong grip. He smiled and looked Jonathan in the eye. "A pleasure to meet ye'."

"And you."

"I can't offer you nothin' stronger to drink than hot water, but it keeps the chill off." Jonathan gratefully accepted.

As the night wore on, they feasted on roasted rabbit, and Jonathan told Boone his entire story: His love of the frontier, his feelings for Nancy, the fool's errand with Isaac, and finally his return to the New River, and the unwelcome surprise that waited for him there.

Boone listened intently, staring into the fire and nodding on occasion. He frowned at Jonathan's recounting of the treatment the people of Cumbow's settlement received at the hands of the wealthier classes and winced when Jonathan told him of Nancy's marriage.

"My wife Rebecca done give up on me two or three times when I didn't find my way home in a timely fashion." He shook his head and grinned ruefully. "I've met Solomon Osborne a time or two. He ain't a bad sort. I know that don't make you feel no better, though."

"If he will take good care of her and treat her right, I suppose that is something," Jonathan admitted, though jealousy still burned in his heart, and the bitter taste of disappointment still soured his tongue.

They talked late into the night, talking about surveying, swapping tales of Indian encounters, and sharing bits of lore, and woodscraft. Jonathan had, of course, previously heard of Daniel Boone, and found the reality of the man to be very much like his reputation. He was plainspoken and sensible. A knowledgeable woodsman, he was humble, yet confident. Jonathan liked him.

"I reckon it's time I turned in," Boone finally said, stretching and yawning. "But first, I want to give ye' something to think on. I know ye' care for that girl, but I believe the two of us are alike. The thing we love the most is the woods. Keep on living for that, and ye' always got a reason to wake up in the morning."

Jonathan bade Boone good night and wrapped himself tightly in his blanket. His heart still ached, but it already felt like an old bruise. He now realized he had something to hold on to, and he knew that somehow, he would be all right.

Chapter 8

May, 1765

"Quiet, brothers. I think I heard something." Enoch waved his hand at Solomon and Ephraim, cutting off their loud talk. He strained to make out sounds in the forest, but if he had heard something, it was gone now.

"What was it?" Ephraim asked. "Some wild Injun woman come to make you her bride, no doubt." Ephraim lay on his side, tossing bits of twig into the campfire. They had been caught in a rainstorm earlier in the evening, and their clothing now hung near the fire to dry. They had whiled away the evening exchanging stories and good-natured banter.

Seated alongside him, his brother Solomon grinned but did not join in the taunts. He was a quieter sort than the other two, and more thoughtful.

"You just go on and laugh if you like," Enoch muttered, peering out into the darkness. He could not see anything, but he was certain that his ears were not deceiving them. "Just go on and laugh."

"Oh, I shall," Ephraim chuckled. "You need not worry about that."

"Perhaps you should not be so quick to make him the butt of your joke," Solomon interjected. "Enoch is not the one who was sitting by the fire with his feet propped up, and shot the toes off his boots when a buck wandered into camp."

To his credit, Ephraim laughed as heartily at the memory of his own folly as he had at Enoch. Their hunt had been a bountiful one and the mood was light.

"Tell us, Solomon," Ephraim said. "What shall you buy for that pretty wife of yours when we sell all of these fine furs?"

"I do not know," Solomon replied, whittling a length of hickory with his hunting knife. "Nancy is with child, and her mood tends to change quicker than the weather. I shall have to think long and hard about it so as not to upset her."

"Well I think," Enoch interjected, "that for my part, I shall…"

His words were cut off as the night erupted in a thunder of gunfire. Musket balls tore through the clearing, sending up sprays of dirt and bits of wood where they struck trees or fallen logs. Enoch dove to the ground and lay flat, looking around for the attackers, who remained out of sight. He turned to Solomon, who lay nearby.

"Who do you think it could..." His words dissolved into a groan as his gaze fell upon his brother's face, the firelight dancing in his lifeless eyes. A trickle of blood oozed from the corner of Solomon's mouth. It could not be.

Enoch crawled over to where Solomon lay, and held his ear to his brother's chest. There was no heartbeat. He held his hand in front of Solomon's mouth, and felt no breath. His brother, his strong, young brother who had a child on the way, was dead.

"Are they gone?" Ephraim cowered in the pitiful shelter of a fir tree, not daring to come out. "Can you see anything?"

As if in answer to his question, another round of shots sounded in the night. A musket ball clipped a limb from the fir under which Ephraim hid, and another struck in the center of their fire, sending sparks flying like shooting stars. With a yelp, Ephraim fled into the night. Their attackers must not have had time to reload, because no more shots rang out. A cloud of smoke, carrying the acrid scent of gunpowder, drifted into the camp like a sinister spirit of death.

Squirming on his belly like a snake, Enoch slithered into the deepest shadows, trying not to make a sound. His mind raced. He was in his night clothing. Everything he had, his horse, his rifle, his provisions, even his boots, all lay near the fire. To return for them would mean moving back into the firelight, thus giving the attackers an easy target.

As if to emphasize this point, they fired another round of shots into the camp. Solomon's lifeless body contorted as he was struck repeatedly.

"Cowards," Enoch whispered, so low that he could scarcely hear himself. "At least be men enough to show yourselves." A stray tear trickled down his face, dripping off his chin. Whether it was sadness at the loss of his brother, or rage at being unable to fight back, he could not say.

He continued to work his way into the darkness, out of the firelight and away from the direction in which he was fairly certain the attackers were hidden. As he watched, he saw a sudden movement. He tensed and held his breath.

Without warning, Ephraim bolted into camp, ripped loose his horse's hickory bark halter that was fastened to a nearby tree, leapt atop his mount, and galloped away. Shots followed him as he went, but Enoch heard no cry of pain or fear. Perhaps his brother had escaped, though recklessly galloping a horse through the dark forest could kill him just as quick.

Shadows crept toward the fire. The attackers must have been satisfied that no one was left alive.

That settled things for Enoch. Even if he could wait them out, they would not leave anything of value behind. He might as well try to make for home while they were rifling through the camp. Refusing to think of the distance or the danger, he set off in silence. A long hunter was now the hunted.

The sound came again, low and mournful. Nancy stoked the fire, as if its warmth could melt the chill from her bones. She had heard stories of haints, spectral creatures that haunted the hollows of the wilderness, and the scriptures told of demons and devils, but she did not believe in such. There were dangers aplenty in the wilderness; dangers that were much more immediate than the imaginings of folklore. Yet, on a night such as this, when the moon cast the world in an ethereal glow, every sound carried a note of fearfulness.

"Uuuuunnnnhhh!" It was not the wind, and whatever it was, it stood right outside her cabin. Something scraped along the ground, coming ever closer to her front door. She had a vision of some shambling beast creeping toward her, and the image, though foolish, frightened her into action.

She snatched the rifle Solomon had left for her, loading it as she had been taught. Its weight in her hands gave her a comfort the fire blazing in the hearth had not. Emboldened, she stepped toward the door.

"Who is there?" She waited for a reply, her hand drifting to her belly in which her child grew. She must keep her baby safe. She would be as brave as she needed to be, no matter how her heart pounded and how much her stomach threatened to sick up. She took a breath and steeled herself so that her voice would not quaver. "Who is there?" she shouted again.

No answer.

She moved toward the door, debating whether or not to pull the latch, throw open the door, and confront whoever or whatever was on the other side. It was a foolhardy notion, but she hated waiting fearfully in her cabin, wondering what was outside. She would rather step out and have it done with, one way or the other.

One thought stayed her hand: Indians. What if a group of savages waited outside, trying to draw her out? She gritted her teeth, gripping the rifle tighter. *One shot.* One shot would not kill a whole band of Indians. Where was Solomon? Why had he not yet returned?

Her fascination with the handsome long hunter had long since faded. He continued to be kind to her, and was a very good provider, but he was a distant man, prone to wander both in body and mind. He lived for the hunt, and each trek kept him away longer and longer. At times, she wondered if some day he might not return at all. Strange, the thought frightened her more than saddened her. She realized now how much she relied on his strength, and the protection he afforded her.

Something scratched at the door, snapping her attention back to the moment. Her first thought was to fire through the door, but something stayed her hand.

"Name yourself, or I shall shoot you where you stand!" She hoped she sounded more dangerous than she felt.

"Nancy..." The voice was weak, little more than a whisper, but she recognized it immediately.

"Enoch!" she cried.

She flung the door open and Solomon's brother tumbled onto the floor. He was filthy, the remains of his night clothes shredded and caked with dirt and blood. He rolled over onto his back and stared glassy-eyed at the ceiling.

"What has happened?" she asked, falling to the floor alongside him and laying a hand on his chest. "Where is Solomon?" Her heart pounded, and a roar set up in her ears as if all the blood in her body were thundering through her like a raging storm.

Ephraim's mouth worked furiously, but his words were a dry, cracked whisper.

Nancy leaned in close, putting her ear next to his lips. She could make out one word.

"Indians."

Chapter 9

April, 1770

Jonathan could not keep the spring from his step as he hopped out of the wagon and moved to help Nancy down. He could scarcely believe how his fortunes had changed in a few short years.

He had thought Nancy lost to him after her marriage to Osborne, and had subsequently hurled himself into his surveying work, and spent the remainder of his time exploring the mountains and forests, more often than not with Duwalla, deepening his acquaintance with the land. It had been a bittersweet time; he dreamed of settling and putting down roots, but the pain of losing Nancy was more than he could bear.

When he finally returned to New River for a visit, he learned of Osborne's death, and hope had returned anew. Nancy had been reluctant at first to renew their courtship, but time and Jonathan's persistence had won her over. In the meantime,

Osborne's son, born shortly after his death, had won Jonathan over. James was now like a son to him, and Jonathan treasured the boy. Jonathan had moved his new family to the Moccasin Valley along with Nancy's brother James Davidson and his family. He looked all around, drinking in the familiar sights as if they were brand new. His heart was full.

"Are there Indians in these parts?" Nancy's eyes darted from left to right, her voice trembling as she spoke. Ever since Solomon Osborne had been killed, she had developed a deathly fear of the native peoples. She now clutched James's hand, pulling him close to her as soon as the boy clambered out of the wagon.

"There is one about." A squat man with graying hair and a deeply lined face sauntered up to where they stood. "Been hanging around here for days. Says he's meeting somebody named Wood." He spat a stream of tobacco juice onto the ground and kicked at it with his worn boot.

"That would be me," Jonathan said. "The name is Jonathan." He offered his hand to the fellow, who gave it a half-hearted shake.

"Ain't none of them Indians any good." Without making an introduction, he turned and wandered away as quickly as he had come.

"Don't you mind old Fugate," a gravelly voice said.

Jonathan turned to see a tall, lanky man with brown hair coming over to greet them.

The man's face was open and friendly and he smiled broadly as he proffered his hand. "The name's McCulloch. Thomas McCulloch." He had a firm grip, and his palm was calloused from hard work.

"You'll find that most of the folks here are much friendlier than Fugate," McCulloch explained. " He's a hard worker, and handy to have around in a fight. On his bad days, though, if he ain't drunk, he's waving his rifle around, or threatening a lawsuit against somebody."

"I know that type," Jonathan said, though in truth, he had spent enough time in the woods that he had blessedly avoided most people like Fugate. "I am glad to hear the others are a friendlier sort. I have actually met a few locals during my surveying. The name's Jonathan Wood. This is my wife Nancy." It still gave him a shiver of joy to introduce her as such. "And this is our son James Osborne. My brother in-law, James Davidson and his wife Catherine will be along shortly. They stopped a ways back to water their horses."

"A pleasure to meet you all," McCulloch said. "We heard tell of your coming. It'll be good to have some more neighbors about. I trust your journey was a safe one?"

"It was most agreeable," Jonathan said. "I've traveled the way alone on horseback many a time, but this is my first experience with a wagon and a family along."

"Folks are finding traveling to be much easier since Daniel Boone widened his wilderness trail," McCulloch said. "He's a good fellow. Have you ever met him?"

"A time or two," Jonathan replied. "He gave me some good advice once, and I shall not soon forget it."

"Have you really met Boone?" James looked up at Jonathan with undisguised admiration. "I didn't know that."

Jonathan nodded, tousled the boy's hair, and smiled down at him, before turning back to McCulloch.

"So, what exactly is the Indian situation at present?"

"Jonathan Wood should be asking *me* that question."

Jonathan smiled at the sound of the familiar voice. Duwalla strode up, grinning at his friend. They clasped hands, and Jonathan turned to introduce Duwalla to his family.

"Nancy, this is my friend Duwalla. I have told you quite a bit about…"

Jonathan broke off as he saw his wife's face grow ashen. He moved quickly to her side and took her by the arm as her legs wobbled.

"Here, sit down," he urged. McCulloch stepped closer, looking concerned.

"No, I am all right," Nancy said taking a breath and pushing his arm away. "James and I shall find a place to get out of the sun."

James waved goodbye to Duwalla as they walked away, but Nancy neither spoke nor met the Indian's eye.

"How about I show the lady and the young man around?" McCulloch said, sensing the awkwardness Nancy's reaction had caused. "I can show them the fort we've just begun building, and the two of you can have some time to visit." He nodded first to Duwalla, and then to Jonathan before hurrying to Nancy's side and offering his arm. She allowed McCulloch to guide her away from Jonathan and the Indian.

"You finally came," Duwalla said with a nod of approval. "How long has it been since you first told me you would settle here?"

"Years," Jonathan said, "but it feels like a lifetime."

"And you finally convinced your woman to marry you, I see."

"It was not easy, I tell you. She was worried about how it would look, and she did not want to dishonor her husband's memory." He shook his head, cutting the toe of his boot into the rich, black earth. The memory still pained him. He had lost her once, and the possibility of her turning him away again had never occurred to him.

"Her brothers in- law were not kind to me at first. One of them even suggested I had something to do with Solomon's death."

"Why would they think that?" Duwalla regarded him with surprise.

"Supposedly, he was killed by Indians, but they never saw their attackers. They knew I cared for Nancy, and that I am a woodsman. Also, it is rumored that I have an Indian friend." He arched an eyebrow at Duwalla.

"Why, what a terrible thing to say about someone."

"Only a foolish man would think that was terrible." They walked along in silence for a while, admiring the beauty of the day and the richness of the land.

"I notice you are still wearing your gorget," Duwalla said, glancing at Jonathan.

Jonathan's hand went to his throat instinctively. The shell gorget was smooth and cool to his touch. He had taken to wearing it after Nancy had married Osborne. He supposed he had been feeling mite inferior after losing her to another man, and the gorget reminded him of another woman—one who saw him as a hero. After a while it had just become second nature to wear it. Now it felt unnatural to be without it.

"You are still thinking about going after that treasure?" Duwalla asked.

"I do not believe your legend that this is a map to any silver mine," Jonathan said. "Most likely, one of your people hid it there to mock the treasure hunters."

"Think as you will. I believe otherwise, though I did not wish to give your cousin Isaac more reason to search for it." He hesitated for a moment. "The legend tells that there is more than a mine there. There is a treasure that white men hid there, but it is forbidden."

Jonathan could not stop his heart from beating a little faster at the thought of a treasure. It was one thing when Isaac had suggested it, but if Duwalla believed it… No. It was foolishness then, and it was foolishness now. He had a lifetime of work ahead of him if he was going to make a home on the frontier for his family.

Duwalla looked up at the sky, where a lone hawk circled on an updraft. "It will do Jonathan Wood no harm to wear his gorget. Any protection he can find will be needed."

"What do you mean?"Jonathan thought he knew exactly what his friend meant, but he hoped he was mistaken.

"Too many English come here." Duwalla's voice was gruff, scornful. "You settle in places meant for hunting. You cut down the trees and drive away the game."

"So your people mean to drive us away?" It was an uncomfortable question, but he and Duwalla had always spoken honestly with one another.

"Not my people. Not right now. But the Mingo are raiding." Duwalla squinted into the glare of the midday sun, and was quiet for a long time. "Somehow, it is strange to hear you call them *my* people."

"Why is that?"

"Duwalla lives in two worlds, Jonathan Wood. The English distrust me because I am an Indian. Indians distrust me because I am friends with the English. I do not truly belong in either place." He shook his head. "I do not suppose you could truly understand."

Jonathan was briefly lost in thought, thinking about what Duwalla said. In a way, he did understand. He had always been out of place among his home and family, preferring the woods and the frontier to so-called civilization. But, being a white man, he did not truly belong in this place. Nonetheless, he intended to make a home here for him and his new family, despite the dangers that might assail them. He did not, however, relish the thought of how Nancy would react when she learned of the peril that loomed on the horizon.

"So the Mingo raids are coming," he said, exhaling a long breath of resignation. "You saw what Nancy is like. What do you advise I do?"

"I suggest that you and the other men get your fort built as quickly as possible."

Chapter 10

July, 1772

Jonathan gazed at the sturdy walls of the modest wooden stockade. Despite the protection it, and another nearby, larger fort afforded the settlers, Nancy's dread of Indians had continued to grow in the time they had resided in Moccasin Valley. Despite Jonathan's constant reassurances, she held on to a fear that, at the worst of times, bordered on panic.

The birth of their son John had provided something of a distraction, but also gave her an added reason to worry for the safety of her family. A few times she had pleaded with Jonathan and her brother for the families to return to the New River, but always changed her mind once her fright had subsided.

Jonathan sighed. He hoped the construction of Fort Houston would give her an added sense of comfort, but it seemed to make little difference. The truth was, there was reason for fear. Rumors of violence toward settlers, and unrest among the native people, had occasionally reached their settlement, though he tried to keep them from Nancy as much as possible. He knew he could not keep the truth hidden from her forever.

"Jonathan! Have you heard?" William Todd Livingston, a man he had known from the New River, hurried up beside him, a look of concern marring his face. "An Indian raiding party has been spotted not far from here. We need to get everyone into the fort as quick as we can."

"That is unwelcome news," Jonathan said. He did not know how Nancy would react when faced with an actual attack. He could only wait and see.

Nancy greeted him with a smile as he entered their cabin. Young John lay sleeping peacefully nearby. Jonathan paused for a moment to at his side. He still could not believe he was a father. For him and Nancy to bring a new life into the world here of all places felt as if they were standing in defiance of all the dangers they faced.

He looked down upon his son through a father's eyes. It amazed him that every time he looked into his son's face, he saw a reflection not only of his own visage, but those of his forbearers. The child had the strong jaw of Jonathan's father, the forehead of his Grand-Poppy, and he also reminded Jonathan of many different family members in small, sometimes indefinable ways. How could so many people be wrapped inside of one miraculous life? And the fact that that life had sprang forth on the frontier only added to the miracle.

"Where is James?" he asked, his thoughts now returning to the present.

"He is just outside. Why?" Nancy asked, her eyes narrowing. She had obviously heard something in the tone of his voice. "What is it?"

Jonathan had been certain he was acting nonchalant, but Nancy had seen right through him.

"Rumors are spreading around the settlement of some Indian trouble. Probably it is of no moment, but we should go to the fort just to be safe."

Nancy blanched, but she otherwise showed no trace of fear. She picked up their baby and called for James in a firm voice. Before Jonathan could say anything, she began giving him instructions about what he should gather to take with them into the fort. He knew better than to smile, and the situation was too serious for levity, but it pleased him to be reminded of what a strong woman he had married. He only hoped he could be worthy of her.

"Do you think we can go out today?" James looked up at Jonathan with hopeful eyes. So much of the summer had been spent inside a safety of the fort that the children were growing unbearably restless.

"We shall have to see." Jonathan said. James was a fine boy, but much too confident and independent for his mother's liking. She always feared that James strayed too far and for too long at a time. Jonathan assured her that a strong, self reliant young man was exactly the sort of person who could thrive in this new land they were making. Nancy always got a sorrowful look in her eyes when he said such things, and Jonathan knew she was thinking of James's father.

"Mister Fraser said that some of the men might go out and tend to the crops for a while. May I go with them? I could help, or I could keep an eye out for Indians. I can whistle real loud. Do you want to hear?" He stuck his fingers in his mouth and puffed his cheeks.

"I will take your word on it," Jonathan said, laughing and holding up his hands as if to ward off the sound. "If I decide it is safe enough to go outside for a while, I shall take you with me."

"Truly?" James's eyes grew wide. "Mother will let you do that?"

Jonathan could not help but laugh again. The boy understood much for one his age. "If I am sure it is safe, I think she will let you go. But if I feel it is not safe, I will hear no argument. Do you understand?"

James nodded.

A cry drew Jonathan's attention, and he glanced up to where James Davidson, watch over the stockade.

"It's Samuel Cowan!" Davidson shouted. "He's coming this way, and the Indians are after him!" Just then, loud cries pierced the air, and a gunshot echoed through the hills.

Jonathan did not hesitate, but snatched up his rifle, which was leaning against the stockade wall, and dashed to the gate.

"Lock the gate behind me if I don't make it," he told Davidson. He unbarred the gate and swung it open as Cowan staggered toward him, ashen faced and blood soaking his shirt. He had taken a musket ball, but no telling how serious the wound was.

Three Mingo warriors were in hot pursuit. Jonathan dropped to one knee, took aim, and fired at Cowan's closest pursuer. It was a risky shot. Had Cowan staggered in the wrong direction, Jonathan might have hit him. Instead, Jonathan's well-placed shot took the Mingo in the chest, and he stumbled to the ground, crying out in pain. Another warrior raised his rifle, aiming at Jonathan, but a shot from the stockade clipped the fringe of his loose-fitting buckskin shirt, and he dove to the ground, his rifle tumbling from his grip.

Cowan stumbled and fell at Jonathan's feet. The third Indian, having apparently expended his last shot firing at Cowan, reversed his grip on his musket, and swung it like a club at Jonathan's head. Jonathan ducked under the swipe and thrust the barrel of his own rifle into the Mingo's stomach. The Indian grunted, and fell face-first to the ground. Jonathan drew his tomahawk and looked around for the other attacker, who had recovered his rifle and was now sprinting toward the woods. For a moment he thought to give chase, but then thought the better of it.

"Get back in here!" someone shouted from the stockade. "I see more coming."

Jonathan pulled Cowan to his feet and helped him back to the fort. Something smacked into the wood of the gate, and Jonathan heard the report of musket fire as he staggered under the weight of his burden. Another musket ball raised dirt at his feet that he stumbled into the safety of the boar, Davidson slamming the gate behind him.

Cowan's wife hurried to his side, helping Jonathan ease the man to the ground. Several women hastily gathered around to tend to his wounds. Jonathan stood to find Nancy staring at him, her eyes wide and her face white as a new snow. He reached for her, and for a moment it seemed that she would pull away, but then she fell into his arms, burying her face in his chest, sobbing.

"Never do that to me again. Please. Never again."

Jonathan held her tight, feeling the warmth of her body, and the softness of her hair. He wanted to comfort her, but more than that, he wanted to protect her.

His gaze drifted to the stockade, where Fraser, Davidson, and Fugate were exchanging fire with the next wave of attackers. There was so much danger here, and only by the actions of brave men could they ever survive. He would protect his family. He could not, however, promise more than that, so he kept his silence.

Chapter 11

November, 1774

A golden sun shone down upon the Virginia mountains, making the trees seem to glow with golden halos against the pure, blue sky. No matter how long Jonathan lived here, he never failed to appreciate the beauty of this land, which had scarcely been touched by man's heavy hand. A man could get lost in this veritable Eden, both in body and in spirit.

He heard a faint rustling in the forest, the sound of hoofbeats, and a horse chuffed somewhere just out of sight. Instinctively his hand went to his rifle, but he relaxed his grip almost immediately. It was still difficult to remind himself that a battle was not constantly at hand. The Indian troubles that had plagued them for so long had subsided, and the settlement was enjoying a time of blessed peace. Nonetheless, he kept a sharp eye on the forest from whence the sound had come. Soon enough, a small group of riders emerged from the trees. Jonathan relaxed. Their anticipated guests had arrived.

The first rider that appeared from within the depths of the forest sat astride a piebald mare, and he sat the saddle as naturally as most men walked. Jonathan recognized the man immediately, and went out to greet him.

The man squinted at Jonathan. Recognition dawned on his face, and he raised a hand in greeting. Jonathan waved back.

Daniel Boone dismounted and led his horse to where Jonathan waited. Fixing him with a crooked grin, he clasped Jonathan's hand. His grip was strong, and the flesh of his palm was like old leather. He looked a bit older than the last time Jonathan had seen him. A few more lines creased his forehead, and age was just beginning to make itself known on his temples and sideburns.

"I sure am glad to see you again," Boone said, his grin blossoming into a full-fledged smile. "I hear you 'uns had yourself a spot of Indian trouble in these parts."

"We saw one or two," Jonathan said, laughing. "How about you? Did any of them cross your path?"

"Oh, I seem to recall a couple of 'em," Boone said, removing his beaver hat and scratching his head in mock-concentration. Boone's traveling companions were waiting nearby, so Boone motioned them on to the fort.

"I also seem to recall you had woman troubles once upon a time," he said. "How did that all work itself out?"

"Just fine, I suppose," Jonathan said. "You were right about me. I do love the land. Of course, I did manage to get the girl as well."

"I heard about what happened to Osborne," Boone said, "and I thought about you. Good to know something good could come out of that."

"It *is* something good. If I could convince her to love the land as much as I do, it would be just about perfect."

"More often than not, a woman will love you and but tolerate the land. That is the best most of us can hope for."

"Anyone ever tell you what a wise man you are?" Jonathan said. "They should make you a judge, or a governor."

"Now them is fightin' words!" Boone laughed as he and Jonathan turned and approached the fort, under the watchful eyes of the other men of the settlement. "My mother, now *she* was the wise one in the family. As for me, I reckon it don't take much wisdom to know not to spit into wind."

Jonathan looked at the stockade as they drew closer. The fort had seen its share of fighting in its short lifetime. The logs that formed the palisade were pockmarked with lead balls, and were scorched in many places from fire arrows. The men had been forced to make regular repairs, and the wall was now a motley assortment of both fresh and aged timber.

"It appears you did have yourself a mess of fightin' in these parts," Boone observed.

Jonathan nodded. As they reached the fort, the other villagers slowly gathered around. Some of the women began to whisper, eyeing Jonathan and Boone.

"He really *does* know Boone." Jonathan did not recognize the voice, though it sounded familiar. "I thought he was just boasting."

"I hear tell that Boone saved a man from Indians during the worst of the fighting," another woman whispered.

Standing nearby, Nancy made an exasperated sound and rolled her eyes. She had been so angry at Jonathan when he risked life and limb to save one of their neighbors, but let another woman try to diminish her husband's heroics…

Jonathan grinned at her. As long as Nancy was proud of him, he did not care what anyone else thought.

"Foolishness," Nancy muttered. "How soon they do forget." Standing there in the midday sun, the crisp November wind blowing in her hair, arms folded, toe tapping with barely-contained impatience, and a half-frown pinching her mouth, she looked as beautiful to Jonathan as she ever had before.

If Boone had heard any of it, he had the good grace to ignore it. He doffed his hat as he approached the gate, and bowed politely to the women.

Old Fugate, as he had come to be known in the settlement, stepped forward to greet Boone.

"It is truly a pleasure to welcome you," he said. "If you don't mind my saying, you are a bit of a hero in these parts. We don't see your like very often."

"I thank you kindly," Boone said, obviously uncomfortable with the praise. "But get to know me a bit better, and I promise you, you'll be much less impressed." He smiled and looked around at the faces of those who now encircled him.

"Besides," he continued, "I hear tell that the Moccasin Valley done had more than its share of heroes. It ain't like the fightin' passed you 'uns by. After we take care of business with the fort, I hope to hear about it. Of course, stories go down a lot better if they come with a hot meal!"

Everyone laughed. The men stood a little straighter, and the women beamed. Boone obviously had a gift for putting people at ease, and winning them over with a laugh or a kind word.

"If the brave men of Fort Houston will kindly assemble outside the gate, I reckon we shall get down to business," Boone said, drawing a sheet of rolled paper from an oilcloth bag slung over his shoulder. "After that, I plan to find a comfortable place to sit and rest my feet, and to impose on your hospitality for a while."

"We are happy to oblige," Jonathan said.

Boone unrolled the document, cleared his throat, and began to read. It was written in official language, and more than a mite boring, but every man stood proud, knowing he had done his duty, and acquitted himself admirably. Finally, Boone came to the end.

"By the authority granted to me by the Royal Governor of the Colony of Virginia..."

Jonathan felt a twinge of discomfort at the mention of the governor. Though far removed from the cities of the east, there rose a sense of disquiet among the mountain people. They had heard of the goings on in places like Boston, and most could identify with the desire for liberty, even if they did not hold the same political leanings. Most of them being of Scottish or Irish descent, though, they had little love for England.

"...and the good offices of Colonel William Campbell, I do hereby discharge the men of this fort from service in the Fincastle County Militia, and I commend you for a job well done."

A cheer went up among the men. Some tossed their hats in the air, and a few fired their rifles. Boone shook each man's hand in turn, saying something complimentary to each of them.

Amidst the tumult, Nancy appeared at Jonathan's side. She wrapped her delicate arms around his waist and squeezed him tight. She beamed at him, her eyes shining with pride and adoration.

"You are my hero," she whispered. Jonathan knew that, whatever the future might bring, he had truly found a treasure in her.

Chapter 12

Duwalla eased into the shadows and looked deep into the forest for the source of the sound he had heard. It was faint, but he was certain it was footsteps. A few moments more, and he could just discern movement, and then a few splashes of color. Shawnee.

Had they been Englishmen, he could have evaded them with ease, but these warriors would not be eluded so easily. In fact, the last thing he needed to do was to give them any indication he had been trying to keep away from them. Taking a deep breath, he stepped out from his hiding place.

Three warriors stopped in midstride, and eyed him with suspicion. One of them stepped forward, his rifle trained on Duwalla, who stood very still, so as to avoid any misunderstanding.

"You come to raid?" The voice was deep, his speech slow and measured.

"Yes," Duwalla replied, knowing any other response would make him immediately suspect.

"Good. You come with us then." The warrior seemed to instantly accept him as an ally. He was either a fool, or had an ulterior motive. "There is an Englishman's farm not far from here." He grinned, revealing canine teeth that had been filed to sharp points.

Duwalla's heart sank. He had hoped to get to Jonathan and warn him of the impending danger before it arrived, but this raiding party was heading directly for his friend's farm. Perhaps he could divert them. Old Fugate lived not far from here. It would not be a kindness to lead the warriors to his home, but Duwalla did not like Fugate, nor did the man have any love for him. But how to divert them without arousing suspicion?

Out of the corner of his eye he studied his new companions. He immediately noticed that each wore some form of bone necklace—a talisman for the superstitious. That could help.

"I do not know if that is the wisest course," Duwalla said, his voice grave. "The Big Man lives in that place."

"How big?" A lean warrior with a prominent chin and dull eyes stopped and turned to Duwalla, his hand reflexively moving to clutch the squirrel skull that hung from a cord around his neck. "As big as a bear?"

"Big strength… power," Duwalla whispered in conspiriatoral fashion. "Even the other English fear him."

"We are not English," the leader snapped. "We have nothing at all to fear." His eyes were wide with anger, but there was something in his clipped command that suggested that he was not as certain as he let on. He strode away, not looking back to see if the others followed.

Duwalla flashed a look of false concern at the other Shawnee, who, after a moment's pause, went after their leader, though at a slower pace than before.

As they drew closer to Jonathan's farm, the warriors began to converse in hushed whispers. Duwalla made a point of fixing a look of fright on his face, and jumping at every little sound. The others laughed the first time, but soon seemed to pick up on his apparent nervousness. As they stepped over a small stream, they disturbed a copperhead, which darted out from under a log and vanished into the undergrowth.

"He goes now to warn the Big Man," Duwalla whispered, making an elaborate gesticulation as if to ward off evil. The warriors all nodded gravely.

"Remember the treasure," the leader whispered, sensing he was losing his followers. "We find his treasure, we can trade it to other English."

Treasure? What was he talking about? Jonathan had no treasure. Then it came to him. *The mine!* It was not the first time someone had heard tell of Jonathan's supposed secret treasure. Even after all these years, the rumors still dogged his trail. Duwalla needed to do something to help the situation, and he needed to do it fast.

"His treasure is not what you think," Duwalla whispered, hoping the cryptic answer would feed the fear he was stoking within his new companions. None replied, but even the leader looked concerned. "I am told he keeps items of dark power that make the spirits do his bidding." He looked meaningfully at each of the Shawnee. "It is a good thing you wear your bones on your necks." He brought his hand to his own neck, then let it fall, sighing dramatically. "I do not suppose you have one for me?"

The others shook their heads, save the leader, who was pointedly ignoring everything Duwalla said.

When they finally reached Jonathan's farm, Duwalla was sweating. What more could he do? If Jonathan was home, was not taken unaware, and did not mistake Duwalla for an enemy, perhaps the two of them could make a fight of it. Duwalla could probably kill one of the men with his knife without the others noticing, but killing two of them was probably the most he could hope for before they shot him. Unfortunately, everything was quiet, and no one seemed to be about.

"Do you hear it?" Duwalla whispered.

"I hear nothing," one of the men muttered, his voice quavering. Then his eyes suddenly widened. "What is that?" He raised a trembling hand and pointed to what was perhaps the most alien sight any of them had ever seen.

Were the situation not so grave, Duwalla would have laughed. Jonathan's smokehouse was an eight-sided monstrosity that had brought him no end of jokes from his fellow settlers. Jonathan said he had copied the style from smokehouses he had seen in the Tidewater. To these tribesmen, it was well beyond their realm of experiences. This was his last chance.

"It is true!" he wailed, staggering back a few steps and raising his hand as if to fend off an attacker. "It is the home of the spirit that guards the Big Man!" At this, everyone stepped back, now clearly uncertain how to proceed.

Duwalla was about to suggest Fugate's farm when, as if they had planned it, a large man with skin of the deepest black appeared from behind the smokehouse, an axe slung over his shoulder. When he spotted the Indians, he immediately began shrieking and waving his axe.

The frightened Indians had seen enough. At the sight of the charging man, whom Duwalla knew to be Jonathan's newest slave, they broke and ran. Duwalla took off in another direction. The cries of the slave reverberated through the forest, growing increasingly desperate.

Duwalla glanced back, seeing the man seated forlornly on a fencepost, waving his arms and shouting.

Poor fellow, he thought. He probably wanted us to take him with us.

Chapter 13

August, 1775

"Mother, may I go outside the fort and play?" James's words were spoken so politely that Nancy almost said "yes" before she remembered where they were.

"Of course not!" she snapped. "You know how many raids there have been. Why do you think we have been forting up all summer?"

"The men said it was safe. They…"

"You are not yet a man. Do you understand me?" Nancy knew she was being harsh, but the very thought of Indians chilled her blood. She tried very hard to abide Jonathan's friend Duwalla, but his presence unsettled her. Ever since James's father was killed…

No. She would not allow her thoughts to stray down that path. Jonathan had always kept them safe, and had kept himself safe as well. She should not worry so.

"Oh, all right," James said glumly, his head drooping and a frown marring his face. "I don't understand why I have to stay inside," he mumbled. "The gates aren't even closed."

"I beg your pardon?" Nancy looked up from the kettle she was tending. "What do you mean by that?"

"The men left the gate open when they went out to play long ball." Clearly he was pleased to divert her anger toward someone else. "They said they hadn't seen any Indians in days, and they were going to go outside…"

"Show me," Nancy said. "And bring your brother with you." The initial flash of hot anger had been replaced by icy fury. She scooped up one-year-old Henry, who was playing on the ground with his three-year-old brother John. James took John by the hand, and they followed behind Nancy as she stalked toward the gate. Just as James had said, it stood wide open.

She did not know if she was angrier at the men for endangering their families for their foolish game, or at herself for being so engrossed in her cooking that she did not notice their absence. That was not exactly true; she was angrier at the men.

Much angrier.

Reaching the gate, she looked out upon an empty clearing. Shouts arose from somewhere just out of sight beyond the trees, so she knew the men were not far away. Still, to leave the fort open and their families unprotected was foolishness of the highest order. She had a mind to walk right over there and tell them exactly what she thought of their childish behavior. She would…

She froze in mid-stride, a smile breaking across her face as inspiration struck. Confused, James stepped back from her as if she had suddenly taken leave of her senses.

"James, take your brothers back inside," she said, gently laying Henry in his arms. "There is something I need to do."

Jonathan leaned back against a stump and enjoyed the warmth of the sun falling on his face. The sounds of his friends running and laughing filled his heart with contentment. His legs were weary, but in a good way. He had not run like that in… he did not know how long. It felt good to be free from the confines of the stockade, and his heart was lighter than it had been in months.

Forting up was not for him. He had come to this land to enjoy the freedom of the boundless frontier; not to be constrained by walls, and certainly not by fear. He smiled as he watched the others dashing to and fro like boys. He…

The sound of gunfire erupted from the direction of the fort. A shrill scream pierced the air, and then more voices joined in. Women screamed, and war whoops filled the air.

Heart in his throat, he sprang to his feet and dashed back toward the fort. The other men were momentarily frozen by surprise, but they were soon hot on his heels. His breath came in gasps, and icy dread hung heavy in his gut. The shrieks continued unabated, lending urgency to his steps as he ran. What fools they had been to leave the fort unattended. He had been so certain that it would be safe.

Beyond the trees a thick cloud of blue smoke hung in the air.

Another shot…

… and another.

Would they be in time? If so, what could they do without their rifles? His hand went to his hip, and he realized that he had not even brought his tomahawk along with him. Cursing himself again, he broke through the trees into the open area where the fort stood, and stopped short.

The women of the community stood outside the open fort. Each held a rifle in her hands, and were… laughing. Some were even pointing at the astonished men. Fugate's wife was so overcome that she knelt doubled-over, her body heaving with mirth. A knot of children stood in the gate, also laughing at their frightened fathers.

Jonathan felt his face grow hot. A quick glance told him that the other men shared in his embarrassment. He supposed it was no more than they deserved. A shamefaced grin crept across his face, and he sheepishly walked toward the cluster of women who were now jeering at their menfolk.

All of them but Nancy.

Jonathan's wife stood at the front of the group, his rifle lying at her feet, one of which was insistently tapping the ground. She held her arms folded across her chest, and her expression could have cracked stone.

He took a deep breath and walked directly toward her. There was nothing he could do except face her anger. He and the other men had acted recklessly, and considering Nancy's fear of Indians, she particularly had cause for fear. He hoped she did not shout at him too much in front of the other families. He would have to call her down if she did, and that would only make things worse later. Besides, he was the one at fault.

Much to his surprise, she did not raise her voice when he reached her. In fact, she spoke in barely a whisper.

"You have," her voice trembled as she spoke, "a responsibility to protect your family." Her eyes, which were always so warm, now burned with anger. "And you left us alone, with no one to protect us."

"Nancy, I…"

"I came to this place, and I remain here against my better judgment, because I love you more than anything," her voice broke, and she let out a small sob. "But I must know that we can rely on you."

Her words cut directly to the heart of all that he had struggled with these many years. His devotion to her was deep, but this land had a hold on him that he could not escape. He had never been able to explain that to her in a way she could understand. If she had her way, she might have them move all the way back to the Tidewater, but Jonathan could never live that life. Besides, if half the rumors he heard were true, war with England loomed just over the horizon, and who could say where safety might lie if that were to happen? In any case, he owed her an assurance that he would be there for her and the children.

"Yes, you can," he whispered. "Until my dying breath I will give all I have to keep you safe." It was easy to say, because it was true.

"Well then," she said, tears forming in the corners of her eyes, "let us hope that dying breath is many years from now."

He drew her close, and held her tight. She was strong, and together they would find their way.

Chapter 14

July, 1776

"I hear tell there's seven hundred of 'em," Hobbs whispered. The young man's eyes were wide with fear, and his knuckles were white as they clutched his rifle. Jonathan laid a hand on his shoulder and gave it a reassuring squeeze.

"All will be well," he whispered. "You are worth at least five Cherokee, and I'm worth a dozen. That only leaves six hundred eighty-three for the rest of the men."

Hobbs smirked, but some of the tension went out of his face. Jonathan did not know the young man well, but he seemed a decent sort. As long as he did not panic at the first sign of fighting, he would be fine.

"It is not much different from shooting rabbits, except your quarry is a much larger target."

"And the rabbits ain't shootin' back."

"Just stay behind cover and take your time when you shoot. As soon as you fire, drop down and move so they can't use the smoke from your rifle to target you." Jonathan had seen more than his share of Indian fighting, though most of it had been from the comparative safety of a fort. He was surprised to find that he felt no fear. He had promised to keep Nancy and the children safe, and fighting off an invading force of Cherokee was part and parcel of that vow. It was simply what had to be done, and he would think no more about it than that.

War had come to America. A little more than a year before, men in the northern colonies had taken up arms against the mother country, and the rebellion had spread throughout the colonies. Here on the frontier, they had thought themselves relatively insulated from the conflict, but the British had taken to inciting the Indians to perpetrate acts of violence against settlers up and down the western border of the colonies. Until now, that violence had amounted to little more than the raids they had been accustomed to, but today was different.

A force of six or seven hundred Cherokee, if the reports were accurate, were moving north up the Great Valley, taking scalps, burning cabins and crops, slaughtering livestock, and generally leaving devastation wherever they passed. Settlers fled their coming, and men from all around the Watauga area had gathered at Fort Heaton to meet the invaders.

The invading force was led by Dragging Canoe, a Cherokee warrior of fierce reputation and remarkable fighting skill. A resourceful leader, he was both cruel and effective, and took great pleasure in the destruction of anything relating to the white man.

The pioneer men had joined forces with a small, established garrison that had sent out a plea for help when news of Dragging Canoe's approach reached them. All told, their fighting force totaled fewer than two hundred men. Given their inferior numbers, they would have much preferred to fight from behind the protection of a stockade, or some other set defensive position. The reality of the situation, however, was that the Indians would simply refuse to confront them behind fortifications, and would go on about raiding the nearby settlements until the men came out to fight.

Knowing this, the men had gone to meet the Indians. The battle would take place on Island Flats, a narrow stretch of bottom land. Ridges to the east and west walled in the so-called gateway to Cherokee country. The way was thick with black oak and dense undergrowth.

The frontiersmen fanned out, their line covering a quarter of a mile or more. At a signal from James Thompson, who commanded their force, Jonathan moved ahead to serve as part of the scouting contingent.

He moved cautiously, creeping forward on the balls of his feet, careful not to make any unnecessary noises. His eyes searched the dense foliage, seeking any sign of movement. All was eerily quiet.

The tangle of forest suddenly opened into a small clearing, slanted beams of afternoon sunlight painting it a dull yellow, revealing a score of Indians moving toward them. They had apparently believed themselves about to catch the frontiersmen by surprise, because shock registered on their faces, and they froze almost as one.

Jonathan dropped to a knee, fired into the midst of the group of Indians, and rolled behind a fallen log. He immediately grabbed his powder horn and prepared to reload. Gunshots and battle cries arose all around him, and a stray arrow sliced the air just above his head, disappearing into the dim woods. With a roar, the line of men for whom he had been scouting charged past, drawn by the sounds of combat. He turned to watch the battle line as it vanished into the thick cloud of gun smoke, sweeping the enemies in front of it.

Feeling a bit safer, he bit off the end of the cartridge, primed the pan of his longrifle, and poured the remainder of his powder into the barrel. He dropped a round ball encased in greased cloth into the barrel and tamped it down. Though no soldier, he was fast; he could reload and fire three and sometimes four shots in a minute.

Before he could join the pursuit, loud cheers erupted in the distance, and soon his comrades at arms came crashing through the woods back in his direction, jovial expressions shining on their faces.

"A good little fight," one man said. Several more nodded and added their agreement. Jonathan was pleased to see that Hobbs was with them, and unharmed. He had taken a liking to the young man. He reminded him of his own stepson, James: a dry wit, perhaps a bit cynical, but a good fellow none the less.

"I expect we're safe for the time being." James Thompson was one of the militia captains, and technically the man in charge of entire force. "This late in the day, I don't expect them to come back. We should head back to the stockade and get some rest. I imagine tomorrow shall be a long day."

It was a relaxed group that made its way back to the stockade. Their first taste of combat, one in which they had not lost a single man, had eased their nerves. For his part, Jonathan was still uncomfortable. They were making too much noise, and paying too little attention to their surroundings. They were ripe for…

Something buzzed through the air like an angry hornet, and one of the men up ahead of him, Logan, he remembered, fell to the ground with an arrow in his neck.

Jonathan whirled about to see an army of Cherokee pouring out of the forest all around them. They looked for all the world to him like an upset anthill. They were everywhere, threatening to devastate all that stood in their paths.

He took careful aim and dropped the first warrior he saw before retreating to a nearby hillock where Captain James Shelby was rallying his men.

The surprised militia men quickly organized themselves into a battle line. They held their ground, and their first round of withering rifle and musket fire shredded the initial wave of the Indian onslaught. Warriors fell shrieking in pain, but they were quickly overrun by the sheer numbers of men that followed them.

The militia line pulled back as they reloaded, and managed another devastating barrage of fire before the attackers were among them. Hand-to-hand fighting ensued, but Jonathan could see little of it amongst the puffs of smoke and tendrils of evening mist. Men locked in combat whirled in and out of sight, in a macabre dance of death.

The men on the hillock kept up a steady fire, targeting the Indians who were hanging back from the fray and peppering the hill with arrows. It seemed to Jonathan that there should be more attackers down below, but the men at the bottom of the hill appeared to be evenly matched with their enemies. His eyes searched the surrounding tree line. Dark shapes, like a low-hanging cloud, circled to the west of their line.

"Over there!" he shouted. "They're trying to encircle us!"

As Captain Shelby barked out orders for the lines to reform, the men re-directed their fire, and began picking apart the flanking force before it could even break from the shelter of the trees. The Indians wavered, but then burst forth from the cover of the forest with bloodthirsty cries, and charged the hillock.

There was no time for organized fire. Every man put lead into the air as quickly as he could. Jonathan got off four shots, but had no idea if any had found their targets. Acrid smoke burned his eyes and throat, and the taste of sweat and gunpowder was thick in his mouth. In the air all about him hung the sounds of fighting and the smell of blood.

He forced his watery eyes to focus, and saw a group of Indians break through the line at the bottom of the hill. The first warrior through was a giant of a man, more than six feet tall and broad of shoulder, wielding a wicked-looking axe. Jonathan drew his tomahawk and dashed to meet him, but another Indian broke through the line and veered into his path. The warrior swiped at Jonathan's neck with his hunting knife, but Jonathan ducked the blow, and clove the man's knee with his tomahawk. As the warrior went down, Jonathan struck him across the temple and the man crumpled to the ground.

He looked up to see the big Indian locked in combat with Robert Edmonson, a lieutenant in the militia. The warrior fought with his axe, and Edmonson with knife and tomahawk. They hurled blows and curses at one another with such ferocity that the battle seemed to slow all around them.

Indeed, many on both sides had paused in fighting and backed away from one another to watch the fight. As the duel spun its way down the slope of the hillock, the Cherokee moved back toward the trees, shouting encouragement to the big Indian, while the militia men gravitated toward the higher ground, seemingly mesmerized by the single combat.

Finally, the Indian overextended himself, taking too broad an overhead stroke. Edmondson met the attack with his own tomahawk, and drove his knife into the warrior's gut. The Indian went limp with shock, and Edmonson wrenched the big axe away from him, reversed it, and crushed the Indian's skull with a vicious blow.

The Cherokee warriors cried out in rage, but the fight was out of them. A final flurry of arrows hissed a defiant whisper, but they were quickly in full retreat. The frontiersmen gave chase, but only to ensure that their opponents were not regrouping for another attack.

Jonathan joined the pursuers, tracking the Cherokee retreat until he and the others were satisfied that the enemy had fled the battlefield. Only then did he allow himself to breathe a sigh of relief. He had survived. He would go home. But would there be more battles ahead? His fingers traced the lines of his gorget as he thought. His dreams of a peaceful life in this beautiful land, of raising a family with the woman he loved, seemed as insubstantial as the wisps of mist rising from the ground. Every time he tried to take hold of them, they slipped from his grasp.

Chapter 15

October, 1780

"So Edmonson says to his nephew, '*I heard you utter an oath during the battle. I shall have to speak to your father about this.*' And his nephew says, '*But Uncle, I heard you swear the very same oaths, and worse, while you were fighting the big Indian.*' Edmonson is a good Presbyterian, and he will hear nothing of the sort. His face turns red and he blusters about for a minute, so I put a hand on his shoulder and I say, '*It's true. I heard you myself. Would you like me to tell you which words you said?*'"

Jonathan smiled and enjoyed the guffaws of the men who stood in a tight circle around him, waiting for orders. Years later, the story was still good for a laugh. Though Indian troubles persisted, the ensuing years had brought no battle like the one at Island Flats. The Revolution continued, however, bringing rumors of pending danger, but little that immediately impacted life on the frontier.

Until now.

Earlier that year, the British had taken control of Charleston, South Carolina and forces under the command of Banastre Tarleton were moving north by northwest, wreaking havoc in the Carolinas. Tarleton had come to be known as "Bloody Ban" or simply "The Butcher" due to the ferocious raids he led, and the recklessness with which those under his command took to killing. His forces had even raided Loyalist encampments by mistake, inadvertently wiping out their own allies in Tarleton's relentless campaign to frighten the countryside out of rebellion. In one notorious battle at the Waxhaw, it was said that Tarleton and his men had slaughtered American soldiers under a flag of truce—even those who knelt with hands upraised. But if Tarleton thought his unique version of giving quarter had demoralized the Americans, he was sorely mistaken. His depredations had only served to strengthen the resolve of the men who resisted the British.

Now, a force of over 1,000 men under the command of Major Patrick Ferguson had encamped in North Carolina, and threatened to control the southern portion of the Great Wagon Road that ran from Philadelphia to Augusta. A British victory would effectively seal off the southern colonies of Georgia, South Carolina, and

North Carolina, and deal a crippling blow to the fight for independence.

Like the "clan calls" of their Scottish forbearers, the men of southwest Virginia and northeast Tennessee mustered at Sycamore Shoals to prepare for battle. There were familiar faces among these mountain men. Jonathan had seen both the younger and older Edmonsons, as well as other veterans of Island Flats. Charles and Robert Kilgore, and several other men from Moccasin Valley were there as well.

The "Overmountain Men", as they were known in the colonies because they had settled on the western side of the Appalachians, had marched for thirteen days to where they now waited to confront the Loyalist forces at King's Mountain.

"It won't be like it was for you 'uns at Island Flats," John Crockett said. Crockett had come to the Watauga area by way of Virginia and Maryland. "You 'uns had fewer men, but you had some high ground. And we ain't fightin' Injuns with bows and arrows. Up there is fighting men with muskets, sitting on top of a mountain." He made this pronouncement without a trace of concern, much less fear, in his voice. It was as if he were simply describing a job that needed doing. Some of the other men looked nervous, however.

"All I see up there is a bunch of treed possum, and it's our job to shoot them down," Jonathan said. "Are you men with me on that?"

"I like your way of thinkin'," Crockett said with a grin, and the others visibly relaxed.

Colonel William Campbell reined in near where they stood, and a cry went up for the men under his command to gather. The colonel, a close relative of Patrick Henry, surveyed them with fire in his eyes and a faint smile on his face.

"The moment is at hand," he proclaimed in a booming voice. "A few of our number have gone over to the other side during the night." A dark murmur filled the gathering of men. "They seem to prefer the company of Major Ferguson and his Tories to that of the brave patriots I see assembled before me. Allow me to remind you of the words of Major Patrick Ferguson, whom we shall engage in battle today.

More than a few curses found their way to Jonathan's ear. The men were all too familiar with Ferguson's words. His threats and blasphemy had stoked the fire ignited by rebellion and kindled by Banastre Tarleton's depredations.

"'I shall lay waste to their country with fire and sword.'" Campbell paused for effect before sharing choice bits of the proclamation, ending with the boast that had most drawn the American's ire. "'Not even God Himself can take me off of this *mountain.'"* At those words, a roar of defiance arose so loud that Jonathan wondered if they could hear it atop King's Mountain.

"I say to you, we are not God. We are merely men. But we are hunters, and that is how we shall fight this battle. Our quarry is there." Campbell pointed to the summit of the mountain. "Remember these words. Remain behind cover, choose your targets with care, and bring them down one at a time. We have no bayonets. If they charge, you retreat to cover and resume firing. Do not assault the summit until the command is given. Am I understood?"

A mumbled assent arose from the gathered forces. Jonathan looked around at their army, in their fringed buckskin hunting shirts, in their coonskin or floppy felt hunting hats. They were not garbed in the finery of a soldier, but each was a good man, a man made hard by life on the frontier. In every face he saw a man upon whom he could rely. Moving with a sense of shared purpose, the Overmountain Men headed to battle.

It was well into the afternoon when the colonial forces began their attack. Divided into nine companies, they encircled the base of King's Mountain and drove for the summit. Jonathan's company was to take the southeastern slope, or the "high heel" of the footprint-shaped mountain. The way was steep and rocky, perhaps the most dangerous ascent of all.

As the first shots rang out, Colonel Campbell, who had thrown off his coat, rode to the fore, shouting, "Here they are my brave boys; shout like hell and fight like devils!" At his words, the men opened up with their rifles, whooping like savages.

Jonathan guided his horse with his knees, keeping his hands free for his rifle. He fired, reloaded, and fired again as fast as he was able. All around him men were on the move, firing from the saddle or from behind rocks and trees; keeping out of the worst of the line of enemy fire, but moving inexorably forward.

A bullet whistled past his ear, and he steered his horse into a thicket of pine, returning fire as he went. Shouts arose from up above, and he saw soldiers charging down the slope, bayonets fixed.

"Retreat!" someone cried out. Jonathan wheeled his horse around and galloped down the slope. Ferguson's troops quickly broke off their assault as the patriots seemed to melt before their eyes, vanishing into the forest at the base of the mountain. As they retreated, the assault resumed, as the Overmountain Men, experienced hunters all, continued to pepper them with rifle fire.

Three times they attacked the slope; three times the Loyalists countered with a bayonet charge. And each time the Loyalists counterattacked, the colonials hastily made a controlled retreat out of harm's way, laying down deadly cover fire and making the Loyalists pay dearly for exposing themselves in the charge. Gradually, their superior rate of fire, accuracy, and ability to fight effectively from behind cover was wearing down Ferguson's forces. Jonathan was put in mind of chopping down a large tree with a dull axe. It was slow work, but it eventually got the job done.

The fighting on the mountainside was some of the fiercest he had ever seen. As they fought their way back up the slope, he saw Lieutenant Robert Edmonson leaning against a tree, having his wounded arm bandaged by Robert Craig. As Craig tied off the bandage, Edmonson, his arm soaked in blood, leapt to his feet and cried, "Let us at it again!" Whooping like a savage, Jonathan put heel to his horse and charged up the hill.

A contingent of Ferguson's forces were firmly entrenched in a rocky outcrop near the summit of the slope, and were making a tenacious defense against the relentless assault of the Virginia men. As a thick knot of attackers kept up a slow frontal attack, Jonathan swung around to the left behind the cover of a thicket of trees, and came at the Loyalists from the side.

His shot took one of the men in the side, and the man fell face-down where he knelt. The soldier beside him did not realize the shot had not come from downhill, and thus did not notice Jonathan until he was almost upon him. Having no time to reload, the man sprang out of the way of Jonathan's charging mount, and thrust desperately with his bayonet. Jonathan only managed to redirect the thrust with his tomahawk. He felt a sharp pain in his neck, but adrenaline would not let him consider it. He struck the man a backhand blow with the flat of his tomahawk, and then rode him down on his way up the slope.

His hand went to his neck and came away bloody. The bayonet had cut him, but it did not seem to be serious. Then he realized his gorget was gone. Between his redirecting the blow and the protection of the shell gorget, his life had been saved. It had seemed almost like a part of him, and he hated to lose it, but that did not matter now.

He reached the summit of the mountain and witnessed a scene that was beyond his worst nightmares. The entire mountaintop seemed to erupt in smoke and fire, so fierce was the fighting. Colonel Frederick Hambrecht, his hat riddled with bullet holes and blood soaking his side, rode past, shouting at the top of his lungs.

Jonathan sprang from his horse and, standing behind it for protection, hastily loaded his rifle.

Resting his rifle on his saddle, he took his time and made his shots count. All around him, the Loyalist forces fell as the colonials closed in. Somewhere in confusion of battle, a white flag went up, but it was immediately yanked down. Jonathan kept firing.

In the distance, he spotted Ferguson, who seemed to have finally realized he was beaten. He dropped down from his own horse, tore off his officer's coat, and pulled a flannel shirt off of a fallen colonial. Not wanting to miss his chance, Jonathan reloaded his rifle as quickly as he could.

Meanwhile, Ferguson, now disguised in the flannel shirt, leapt astride his horse. Flanked by a pair of his officers, they galloped directly toward Jonathan's position. Jonathan took aim, and squeezed the trigger. Ferguson spun from his saddle and fell hard to the ground.

The battle continued unabated. Jonathan remained behind the scant protection of his horse, his rifle propped on his saddle. It steadied his aim, but also helped in holding back the fatigue that threatened to overwhelm him. He continued to fire at the thinning Loyalist force. Another white flag was raised, but the man was immediately shot down. Jonathan winced. This was not the honorable way to fight.

Voices arose from the din, desperate voices begging for mercy and offering to surrender.

"Give 'em Tarleton's quarter!" one man yelled. Others took up the cry as the battle continued. A loyalist turned and took aim at Jonathan, who ducked a moment too late.

The world exploded.

Chapter 16

"Where are you taking us?" The prisoner's voice was bitter and resentful He scowled at Jonathan, who stood guard over their group. "Or are you just going to kill us?"

"No one is going to be killed," Jonathan said, though he could not say for certain that his words were true. Already there was a strong sentiment among those who remained to escort the prisoners to the Continental Army jurisdiction in Hillsboro that the so-called "Loyalists" should be hanged as traitors. Considering what Ferguson had done to the Americans at Waxhaw, many thought it the just thing to do. Jonathan hoped the Americans kept themselves under control until they reached their destination, where justice could be meted out in proper fashion.

He rubbed at his eyes, which still burned from the injury he had sustained in the battle. If one could call a musket ball striking your bearskin saddle blanket and blowing dust and debris into your eyes an 'injury'. He had endured a few japes at his expense, but everyone knew he had given as well as he had got and more in the fight, so he took it all in stride.

The battle had continued only a few minutes after Ferguson was killed. His body had been defiled in ways Jonathan did not like to think about, and he was grateful that in his half-blinded state he had not seen it happen. There was honor in their victory, but not in some of the men's conduct after the battle. He supposed that was at least part of why he had volunteered to escort the prisoners. Perhaps he could help cooler heads prevail.

"I know you," the prisoner whispered in a tone of surprise.

"Of course you do. I'm the man whose army just licked you."

"No… I know you from before. You're that cousin of Burwell's; the one that took up for that half-breed girl."

Jonathan regarded the man through new eyes. The man's distinctive chin, long and a bit out of place from the rest of his face sparked his memory. Oh yes, he remembered Augustine Hobbs.

"I still have a scar thanks to you," the man said, pushing back his sleeve to reveal a puckered, pink scar marring his forearm. "I vowed I'd make you rue the day you ever laid a hand on me."

"Well, you've done a fine job of it so far," Jonathan retorted. He did not want to be drawn into words with this man, but he could not seem to help himself.

"Oh, the song isn't sung yet, mountain man. Grimes! You remember this fellow?" The other man with whom Jonathan had fought so many years ago at the end of his failed adventure with Isaac came over to stand next to Hobbs.

"I certainly do," Grimes said. His blond hair was caked with dirt and blood, and his fine clothes were torn and filthy. "What are you doing out here? Shouldn't you be off somewhere spending your fortune?"

"Did I hear somebody say 'fortune'?" A bear of a man wearing mismatched, ill-fitting clothing that looked like it had once been of high quality sidled up to them. "That is just my game." He leered at Jonathan, his smile at odds with whiskey-colored eyes that oozed evil.

"What do you want, Harpe?" Hobbs would not meet the newcomer's eyes, and both he and Grimes appeared discomfited at the man's presence.

"I want to hear about the treasure. Micajah Harpe likes treasure."

"Well, you'll just have to ask Mister Jonathan Wood about that. He knows the way to Swift's Silver Mine. I'd imagine he has already made away with enough silver to buy a plantation. Then again, he would be back in the Tidewater living like a gentleman if that were the case."

"I have seen what passes for a Tidewater gentleman, and how they conduct themselves," Jonathan said. "I don't think I'd much care to be called one. And there is no treasure. Isaac took me on a fool's errand."

"I don't reckon I'd admit it either if I knew the way to a treasure no one else has ever found," Harpe said, stroking his chin. "Yes sir, you and me need to talk some more about this treasure."

Jonathan was spared further conversation as a clamor arose nearby. He turned to see two men, their hands bound behind their backs, being hauled toward a stately oak tree.

"You cannot do this to us!" one of the men shouted.

"You were tried and found guilty! Now shut your mouth and accept your just consequences." The resentment that had been brewing in the hearts of the Americans since the beginning of the war, and particularly since Ferguson's incendiary proclamation, had finally boiled over.

Jonathan dashed over to the throng that milled around the bound prisoners. He tried to force his way through, but the mass of bodies was too thick.

"Stop this!" he cried. "They must have fair trials!" No one could hear him over the tumult. A rope was slung over a high-hanging branch, and the onlookers cheered as the first man was strung up.

"This is not right!" he shouted, knowing his protestations were futile.

"They're traitors," the man next to him snarled. "They changed sides before the battle. They have it coming to them."

Jonathan shook his head. He could see already that there was nothing he could do to put a stop to this. He was sickened by what he saw, but he could not look away as the second man was hauled up, his feet kicking in frantic desperation, and his bowels and bladder releasing. His struggles seemed to go on forever, but finally he fell still. It was not over, however. Seven more men were now being dragged through the crowd, their eyes wide with fear.

Jonathan had seen enough. Sufficient numbers of men remained to finish escorting the prisoners to Hillsboro—assuming there were any prisoners left to be escorted by the time the mob was finished with their so-called justice. He was going home.

He had gathered his few belongings and saddled his horse when Robert Young hailed him. His surname notwithstanding, Young was older than most of the men who had come to fight, but he had acquitted himself well. He was a good aim, and never panicked.

"You leaving?" the grizzled man asked, not looking at Jonathan.

"I am. What we did on that battlefield was right and just. What they are doing now…" He could not finish his sentence.

"I hear you," Young said. "I reckon I'll see this out 'til the end, but then I'm for home myself." He clasped Jonathan's hand and bade him to be safe on his journey, before adding a word of advice. "Keep a close eye out for the Harpes when you go. They just escaped. I wouldn't want to run afoul of them two while I was all alone. Mean as snakes, they are."

"There are two of them?" Jonathan had disliked Micajah on site, and did not relish the thought of another Harpe.

"Micajah and Wiley. Big Harpe and Little Harpe, they call 'em. They claim to be brothers, but I hear tell they're really cousins or some such. I don't reckon it matters much. I'm happy to see 'em go, to tell you the truth. Hopefully the Injuns will get 'em. Just wanted to warn you, that's all."

"I appreciate it," Jonathan said. "I plan on keeping to myself until I get home." He swung into the saddle and took a long, last look at the encampment. "I believe I have about had my fill of soldiering."

"By the way, Wood" Young grinned at Jonathan. "You know it was really me and Sweet

Lips what shot Ferguson, don't you?" He patted his rifle with obvious affection.

Jonathan smiled. "Tell me, what kind of man gives his wife and his rifle the same name?"

"That is true. Women are twice as dangerous, and ten times more unpredictable than a rifle. I'll have to give the wife another name."

Jonathan laughed and doffed his hat to Young. He wheeled his horse and put heel to its flanks. Soon, he had left the encampment far behind, and was at home again, alone in the woods.

Chapter 17

"Someone's coming! They're coming!" The shouts echoed through Fort Houston.

Nancy dropped the bundle of firewood and dashed to the gate. The locals were gathered at the gate, looking out at the group of approaching riders. There had not been any Indian attacks of late, nor signs of the British in Moccasin Valley, but with so many of the men away, it had seemed prudent to fort up until their return.

Nancy watched as the shadowy group of riders drew closer, and each became recognizable. Her heart fell. She saw that Jonathan was not among them. Perhaps he had been delayed, or was simply lagging a little farther behind. She kept watching the forest behind them, hope draining slowly away as she saw no one else.

The lead rider, Charles Kilgore, his arm heavily bandaged, dismounted. Pushing past the other women, Nancy rushed over to him.

"Where is Jonathan?" she asked. Part of her did not want to hear the answer, and when he looked at her, she was even more certain she would not like what he had to say.

"I do not know," he said. His voice spoke of a weariness that was bone-deep. "I saw him fall during the battle, sometime toward the end. There was a puff of smoke and he fell. Then, one of the Tories came charging at me, and I lost sight of him. I could not find him after that. I wish I could tell you more, but I just do not know. I am truly sorry." He looked away, clearly not relishing being the bearer of bad news.

Nancy's strength failed her, and she sank to the ground, trembling. She clutched her arms to her chest as if she could stop the trembling. She felt like she was going to freeze to death. She was drifting. It was all so unreal.

She had long feared this day would come—the day she lost another husband. What was she to do? Return to her family? This was a dangerous time to be traveling anywhere. But how could they survive on the frontier without Jonathan?

Kilgore knelt beside her, and the others circled around. They looked at her with sympathetic expressions, but they were of no comfort to her. She did not want their pity.

"It is possible," Kilgore began, measuring his words with care, "that he is still alive. It was all very confusing. Just as the battle ended, another British contingent arrived. They did not know the fight was over, and they attacked. We fired back at them, and the battle almost started all over again. All of it was... chaos. Soon after, some of the men were dispatched as messengers, and others were rounded up to help escort the prisoners..." He looked up at the sky as if the answer hung there amongst the clouds. Finally he shook his head.

"I wish I could tell you more, Nancy. I truly do. But don't give up hope just yet." He gave her a sympathetic pat on the shoulder and went to join his family.

If there had been no one else about, she might have been tempted to lie down and not get back up again, but pride, obligation, and a burning desire to have a definitive answer brought her to her feet. She stood, brushed herself off, and straightened her dress, hoping to salvage what little dignity she had left.

"I have to find out," she whispered. "I have to know if he is alive. If there is any chance at all..."

An idea came to her in a sudden bolt of inspiration, but the very thought of it sent chills down her spine. Duwalla, that Indian friend of

Jonathan's, had been spending time around the fort, asking after Jonathan and doing some trading. None of the men of the Moccasin Valley could be asked to make the dangerous trek into war-torn territory, but perhaps the Indian would do it. Jonathan and he had formed a bond that she had never understood. She didn't trust him any further than she trusted any other savage, but sometimes you had to work with the tools at hand.

Duwalla was en camped a short walk from the fort. James went along with her. The young man looked up to the Indian almost as much as he looked up to Jonathan. Nancy had reminded him on many occasions that it was Indians who had killed James's father, but it mattered not a whit to him.

"Indians killed my father, but not *that* Indian," he always said.

Some of the more suspicious types in the New River had intimated that Jonathan, jilted by Nancy, had used his friendship with the Indian to have Osborne killed. Nancy had never believed it, and she had it on good authority from several reliable men that neither Jonathan nor Duwalla had been anywhere near the New River for months before or after Solomon's death. Still, Nancy simply did not trust Indians. The truth was, she feared them now just as much as ever. Even Duwalla.

She found Duwalla lounging against the bole of a pine tree, sharpening his knife with a stone. His horse was tied to a nearby tree, and was cropping at the sparse grass. Duwalla smiled as James approached, but stole a suspicious glance at Nancy. He did not stand to greet her, as a proper man would have, nor did he give her any word of welcome. He simply stared at her with an expectant look on his face.

"We have come to ask for your help," James said. "We…"

"Be still, James. It is my place to ask." Nancy tried to keep her voice from quavering. She was shaking inside, but she had steeled her nerves for this encounter.

"Jonathan has not come home from the battle." There! She had managed to say it without so much as a tremor in her voice. "We have reason to believe he might still be alive, but we do not know where he is."

She paused, hoping Duwalla would fill the silence with an offer of help, or at least a word of sympathy, but he did not. He was, however, looking her in the eye and listening intently. That was a good sign, at least.

"I have come to ask if you… would you…" She took a deep breath. "Would you please go and see if you can find him, or at least get word of what has happened? He thinks so highly of you, and I know…" She could feel her face turning red, and she hated herself for it. "I know we can trust you."

Duwalla sprang lightly to his feet with the grace of a cat. His eyes remained fixed on hers, and there was a faint trace of a smile on his face.

"Jonathan is my friend. I am glad that you asked me. I shall go." He offered his hand to her, but she froze, unable to take it. Instantly noticing his mother's discomfort, James took Duwalla's hand in both of his and shook it vigorously.

"Thank you so very much," he said. "I told Mother she was right to ask you."

"It was her idea?" Duwalla arched an eyebrow at Nancy.

"Yes," she said, embarrassed at her behavior moments before. "You were the first person I thought of. We can pay you a little…"

"Friends do not ask for payment," Duwalla said flatly. "I will find Jonathan, and I will bring him back to you." That apparently was the end of the conversation, because he turned his back on them and began packing his horse.

She did not know if it was residual fear, or a sense of obligation, but Nancy waited there with James until Duwalla finished his preparations, mounted his horse, and rode away. James waved goodbye to his friend. For her part, Nancy stood with her arms folded across her chest, her flesh a mass of goosebumps. She watched as her unlikely ally vanished into the woods.

Chapter 18

James was stacking firewood behind their home when he heard soft hoofbeats and the nicker of a horse. "Jonathan!" he cried. He had come home! Letting the load fall to the ground, he dashed around the side of the cabin, but came skidding to a halt before he reached the front.

Two men approached in the distance. One was a large, surly-looking sort, while the other was tall and skinny with a sour face. Both were armed, and both were strangers. Immediately sensing something was wrong, he hurried to the back of the cabin and called softly to his mother.

"Someone is coming," he told her.

The look in his eye must have been enough to let her know something was amiss.

"Take your brothers and your sister and hide," she whispered.

James scooped up baby Polly and took the hand of young Jonathan II and hurried out the back. Nine-year-old John and seven-year-old Henry were playing nearby. James ushered them into the barn, where they hid in a stall. He handed Polly over to John and admonished them all to remain silent. Due to the frequency of Indian raids, the older children had made a game of hiding in silence, until they had finally developed such self-control that they could be as quiet as mice. Even young Jonathan II was beginning to understand the game. James only hoped that little Polly would not suddenly decide to become cranky.

His heart racing, James crept to the barn door and looked around, but there was no sign of the men. He quietly made his way to the back of the cabin and peered in the window to his parents' bedroom. He could see through the bedroom door and out into the front room.

As he watched, the front door flew open with a loud crash, and the two men he had seen earlier sauntered in. His vision was limited, but he could see his mother standing stock-still in the bedroom. The gun was in the front room, where the intruders now stood.

"Afternoon, Ma'am," the big fellow said, taking off his cap and bowing to her. Behind him, the skinny fellow snickered. "My name is Micajah Harpe, and this is my brother Wiley, though most just call us 'Big' and 'Little' Harpe. We are looking for Mister Jonathan Wood."

"He is not here," Nancy said. "He was killed at King's Mountain."

Why was she saying that? James did not understand what was happening. Feeling more helpless than he ever had in his life, he held his breath and watched.

"Is that what you heard?" The big fellow smiled, but it was the smile of a predator stalking its prey. "Well, I can tell you that I have seen him with my own two eyes, and he is right as rain. Or, at least he was when I last saw him, which was well after the battle was over. I imagine he shall be home shortly, unless he has gone off to pay a visit to his silver mine."

"He has no silver mine," Nancy said, her voice trembling. "That was nothing but a legend, and his fool cousin tricked him into believing it. In any case, that was many years ago. The silver mine does not exist."

"I beg to differ with you, Ma'am. I believe it does exist, and I know for a fact that he found something on that trip that shows the way to the mine. I see that he has done well for himself. Plenty of land, a right fancy smokehouse, and of course, a beautiful woman." He leered at Nancy and stepped closer to her. His voice dropped to a whisper. "Now tell me; where does he keep his silver?"

"There is no silver." Nancy's voice grew stronger as she spoke. "Jonathan holds county office. He is a surveyor, and he works hard to care for our farm. If we have anything, it is because he has worked hard."

"I see you don't have any children," the man said. "Perhaps you are in need of some assistance in that area." He leaned in close to her, bringing his pockmarked face close to hers, and ran a scarred hand down her cheek.

Nancy shuddered and jerked away. "Do not touch me."

The man slapped her with casual indifference. She staggered back against the wall, holding her cheek.

James's eyes burned with unshed tears. He wanted to scream at the man, to pummel him, but he knew his best efforts would be nothing against this fellow who was all muscle, scars, and greasy hair. The man scared him.

"I am disappointed in your response," the man said, "but not surprised, I do confess. He sat down on the bed, drew a knife, and began scraping dirt from under his filthy fingernails. "It appears that our only remaining option is to wait here for Mr. Jonathan Wood to return home. We will take him by surprise, torture the location of the mine out of him, and then, of course, we will kill him and take the mine for ourselves. Unless, that is, you happen to remember where the mine is located." The knife froze as he studied Nancy.

"I still say there is no mine," she said, "but I think I can give you what you want."

She made her way slowly to the front room, where the skinny man waited. James strained to see what was happening, but all he could make out was the skinny fellow, rifle in hand, blocking the front door.

"Don't ye' try to run now," the skinny one said, his voice high-pitched like a crow. "Micajah don't like it when women don't do what he pleases. He gets downright angry, he does."

"Hush now, Wiley," the big fellow, Micajah, chided. "I have every confidence that this fine woman is going to help us just like she said she would."

Nancy returned to the room clutching the family Bible. Micajah looked at her as if she were crazed, but before he could protest, she opened to the back of the book, tore out the last page, and handed it to him.

James could not see what was written on it, but it made an impression on the big man. His eyes widened, and he bit his lip as he gazed intently at the paper.

"What is this?" he asked, his voice hollow with suspicion.

Nancy took a deep breath and let it out before she answered.

"Jonathan did bring something back from that fool trip. It was just an old Indian trinket, but this was carved onto the back. It seemed special to him, so I copied the carving into the Bible.

"What about the writing?"

"I sometimes wished we had the money to go back to Tidewater," Nancy blushed and hung her head at this admission. "So I would look at Jonathan's maps, and try to make sense of the markings. I don't know if the places I wrote down are the right ones or not. It was just a way of making myself believe we could get away from the Indians some day." She raised her head and stared at Micajah, her face a mask of defiance. "I still think it's a legend, but if you're fool enough to believe in it, be my guest. Just leave Jonathan alone."

A deathly silence filled the room as Micajah stared down at the paper. Finally he looked up at Nancy.

"You know your letters?"

"Yes," she said, her tone suspicious and fearful. She could not very well deny it after the story she had just told.

"That is just fine, then," Micajah said, rising to his feet and tucking the paper into his belt. "You are going to help make Micajah Harpe a rich man." With a quickness that belied his bulky frame, he snatched Nancy by the arm and dragged her from the room. She screamed and beat at his shoulders and chest, but he seemed not to notice.

James's mouth was frozen in a silent scream as he watched his mother being taken away. He should find their rifle, chase down the men, and shoot them. He should find a knife. He should…

Frozen by fear and helplessness, he sank to his knees and cried.

Chapter 19

Jonathan knew something was wrong the moment he saw McCulloch galloping toward them. He reined in and let his neighbor come to him, dreading whatever it was the man had to say. He had been so pleased when Duwalla had found him on the way back, and even more so when he learned that his friend had come at Nancy's request. Perhaps a thawing of the ice was finally at hand for the two of them. But now, that ice was firmly set in Jonathan's stomach as he read the concern on McCulloch's face.

"Jonathan," he said, nodding at Duwalla before continuing. "It's Nancy. She's been taken."

"Taken?" His mouth was suddenly dry as a desert, and he struggled to form the words. "How? Was it the Shawnee? The Mingo? What happened?" In the back of his mind, he had feared an Indian raid might strike the valley while most of the fighting men were away, but he had not truly believed it would happen.

"It was not Indians," McCulloch said. "Two men took her. Two white men. James saw it happen. He said their names were Micajah and Wiley Hart, or something like that."

"Harpe," Jonathan breathed, remembering the prisoner who had seemed so interested in the legend of the silver mine, and the rumor that Jonathan held the key to the mystery. He had thought nothing of it when he learned the Harpes had escaped. They must have made straight for Moccasin Valley.

"But why did they take Nancy? Unless they want to use her to make me show them the way. But I don't know the way. I don't even have…" His hand strayed to his throat, feeling the conspicuous absence of the gorget.

"According to James, Nancy gave them a map. Said she had copied it into her bible from something or other you found once upon a time. It's all a very strange story, but suffice it to say, these men took the map and Nancy."

"Where are the children?" Duwalla interjected. "Did the men take them as well?"

Jonathan's mind continued to spin out of control. The shocking news seemed to have deprived him of rational thought. If the Harpes had harmed his children…

"The children are safe," McCulloch assured him. "We are taking care of them. James did a fine job of keeping them hidden, and then getting them safely to us." He shook his head. "I simply cannot imagine a lad his age having to watch something like that and still being able to take care of his brothers and sister. He is a fine boy."

"That he is," Jonathan said, trying to regain control of his thoughts. "So the Harpes are on their way to look for the mine, and they have taken Nancy with them. I have to get her back." He turned to Duwalla.

"You do not have to ask, my friend," Duwalla said, his voice solemn. "She has no love for me, but Jonathan Wood loves her, and that is enough. We will go together."

"William Houston's got a dozen men making ready to set out after them," McCulloch said. "I was told to head toward King's Mountain, and if I found you, try and catch up with the others."

"No," Jonathan said. "That many men would draw attention to themselves. Harpe is pure evil. He would cut Nancy's throat just to spite me. Duwalla and I can track them better than anyone else, and we can do it without being seen."

"Are you sure that is what you want to do?" McCulloch asked. "Fifteen men can put up a better fight than two."

"It will be like stalking a deer," Duwalla said. "Or perhaps a bear, if the tales Jonathan told me on our ride back from King's Mountain about the big man is true. We will make no more sound than a shadow makes as it passes across the ground. We will find them."

"Tell James I'll bring him back a scalp or two," Jonathan said, rage boiling inside him as the reality of Nancy being in Harpe's clutches finally took hold. "And tell the children that I love them, and that I shall have their mother home to them safe and sound. I promise."

McCulloch gave them instructions on where to pick up the Harpes' trail, and soon he and Duwalla were on their way. As they rode, he kicked his horse into a gallop, seeking to outrun the specter of fear that threatened to overtake him. He would find Nancy. Nothing else mattered any more.

Nancy worked at the ropes that bound her hands and feet, but they would not budge. Micajah Harpe had bound her up tight, and had tied another rope from her arm to his. It would not be easy to get away. Every muscle and joint screamed in agony. Her legs were so numb that she likely would be unable to get very far even if she did manage to work herself free. She sighed and continued to wriggle her wrists.

All around her, the forest was alive with the sounds of night creatures. She found comfort in the wild symphony. The fool Harpes had gotten so drunk that Chief Benge himself and a whole passel of his Cherokee could march straight into their camp and kill them all before the men could wake. The cacophony of creatures indicated that no one approached. Of course, if Jonathan was to come for her…

She could not entertain such a desperate, foolish thought. She did not even know for certain that her husband was alive, and if he was, how long would it be before he arrived home and learned of her capture? In any case, Harpe had vowed he would kill her at the first sight of Jonathan's face. How had things come to this point?

She cursed herself thrice for a fool. She had told Jonathan that she disapproved of his search for Swift's silver mine, and of the very thought of him ever renewing the search, but that had not been entirely true. She had resented Jonathan's original search for the mine because of what it had done to the two of them. It had kept him away from her for so long that she, not knowing the reason for his absence, had questioned whether or not he truly loved her.

That winter, when Jonathan did not return as he had promised, she had finally concluded that she had been jilted; that Jonathan had chosen his beloved woods over her.

The bitter disappointment allowed Solomon Osborne to make a place for himself in her heart. She had married him, and then Jonathan had returned, leaving her torn between two men for whom she truly cared: Osborne, the strong, kind man who was good to her when she was feeling low; and Jonathan, her first and one true love. Little wonder the sight of Jonathan's gorget had always brought about bitter memories of loss.

She had not lied to Harpe about the map. When Jonathan took her over the mountains, and deeper into Indian country, the silver mine had become a fantasy to distract her from the fear that sometimes threatened to overwhelm her. She worked on the map and imagined Jonathan someday finding it and making them rich. They would live in Tidewater splendor and… that was where her imagination failed her.

The truth was, Jonathan's love of this untamed land had infected her a long time ago. The peaceful times when Indian troubles were far from her mind were some of the happiest times of her life. The woods enveloped her like a mother's comforting arms, and the way the morning sun set the mountaintops afire was a testament to God's majesty. This was truly her home as much as it was

Jonathans, and if he could bring her home, she would be the wife he truly deserved.

But first, she had to get away from the Harpes.

Chapter 20

"Something moves across that ridge line," Duwalla whispered. "It is not an animal. I saw a flash of metal."

Jonathan eased down from his horse and secured it to a nearby tree. Duwalla did the same. They would proceed on foot from here, for they could not risk Harpe hearing their approach and harming Nancy. Jonathan did not doubt the man would do so. His brief meeting with the man was sufficient to convince Jonathan that Harpe was as wicked as they came.

Jonathan had believed himself an expert tracker, but Duwalla put him to shame. The Indian did not miss a single sign of their quarry's passing. Every bent twig, upturned leaf, and scuff mark caught his eye. Together they managed to follow the trail deep into the night, with only the faint moonlight that trickled through the trees, casting shadows like beastly claws onto the gray-brown ground. By its silvery glow they managed to find enough sign to continue whittling away at the Harpes' head start, which was doubtless not as great as the kidnappers assumed it would be. Jonathan wanted to continue their pursuit through the night, but Duwalla pointed out that they would need to be rested for their confrontation with Nancy's abductors, which would likely come on the morrow.

Reluctantly, Jonathan had conceded. He was certain he would be unable to sleep, but weariness from his journey overcame him almost as soon as he closed his eyes.

He dreamed dark dreams of death and loss. While he slept, he found and lost Nancy again and again. He rescued her, only to lose her to Indians; he caught up to her, only to have Big Harpe shoot him in the gut and carry Nancy away as he lay dying; he rescued Nancy, only to have her tell him that she had fallen in love with Harpe; Solomon Osborne returned from the dead to steal her away, accusing Jonathan of foul murder; and worst of all, he found Nancy, only to have Harpe…

He would think no more of that dream, nor any of the others. After a few restless hours he awoke with a strengthened resolve, and he would let nothing stop him from bringing his wife home. Nothing mattered anymore but her. He would take her back to Moccasin Valley, the Tidewater, or he'd even hire a boat and take her all the way back to Scotland if that was what she wanted. He loved this land; but in the face of losing Nancy, he finally realized that love paled alongside what he felt for his wife and family.

He and Duwalla smeared black earth over their hands and faces to better hide themselves in the forest. Many trees were already bare, but sufficient cover remained to conceal their approach. They would have to move quickly on foot to keep up with their mounted quarry, but at the same time be careful enough to escape notice. Fortunately, the way up ahead was steep and would be slow going for the horses.

Duwalla circled wide to the left, moving quickly in search of an ambush site. Jonathan would come in from behind. The plan was a simple one: they would try and make the Harpes believe they were being attacked by Indians, in which case they would have no reason to hurt Nancy — and might even protect her.

Duwalla would use his bow and arrow instead of his rifle. The bow's limited range would not put them at a disadvantage in these tight quarters, and the speed and silence with which he could attack would actually be of benefit.

Duwalla would put as many arrows into the air as he could without endangering Nancy, and Jonathan would charge in, getting Nancy away as quickly as possible. Both of them would whoop and send up Indian war cries as they fought. If all went well, by the time the Harpes realized it was Jonathan who attacked them, it would be too late for them to harm Nancy. It was a good plan.

He said a small prayer and moved in for the attack.

Nancy was tired of Harpe's damp, sour whiskey breath on her neck. She felt hot and itchy, despite the cold November air. In fact, she was feeling downright irritable. She wished her hands were free so she could pull his knife from his belt and stab him right in his gut with it.

She had never seriously contemplated killing another human being, but she would kill both Harpes without compunction if she could. Of course, she couldn't. Her wrists were bound together, and another length of rope ran from her wrists to Micajah's left arm. She rode in front of him, where her every move was visible. Helplessness threatened to overcome her, but she forced it down. She would survive somehow.

She surveyed the forest in front of them. They were climbing a steep slope. Up ahead, the path curved to the right, and the ground to the left fell away in a twenty foot drop onto solid rock. She shuddered and leaned a little to the right, as if she could keep from falling. Her eyes drifted up the hill to a patch of juniper, and something drew her attention. At first, she thought it was only a shadow, but she soon made out the dark outline of a figure hiding among the gray-green of the bushes. As she watched, the figure raised up, the greenery parting as he drew back on a bow.

"Indians!" she shrieked. Panic surged through her, and she flung herself off of the horse. The rope binding her to Harpe grew taut, and the surprised man, still groggy from his heavy drinking the night before, tumbled from the saddle as an arrow sliced through the spot occupied by his head only moments before.

War whoops filled the air, and Nancy screamed and kicked at Harpe, as if she could somehow break away. The big man bellowed and struck her across the temple, but she barely felt it. Another arrow sliced through the brim of Harpe's hat. His hands frantically searched the ground for his rifle, but it was still with his horse, which was now galloping away.

Behind them, Wiley Harpe fired off a wild shot in the direction from which the arrows had come. He was answered by an arrow that took him in the shoulder. He cried out in pain, and his rifle fell to the ground, just as another gunshot sounded from down the hill below them. The lead ball tore through the puffy sleeve of Wiley's coat. He looked around frantically, pausing only to flash a helpless look at his brother before ducking down low and spurring his horse forward.

Micajah drew his hunting knife and raised it high. As he brought the blade down, Nancy was sure he was going to kill her; but instead he sliced through the rope that bound them together. Without so much as looking at her, he sprang to his feet and took off after his brother.

An Indian came dashing up the hill in hot pursuit, his face a dark mask of rage and his eyes afire. In his right hand he held a tomahawk, and in his left a wickedly curved knife. Nancy cringed and pressed herself against the rocky slope as if she could vanish from sight. The Indian was only feet from her when she realized…

Jonathan!

He dashed past her, not even sparing her a glance.

"Harpe!" he cried, barreling toward the big man. She had never heard a man utter such a sound. It thundered with ferocity and righteous rage, filling the forest with its violent tenor.

Harpe whirled around to meet him, as another arrow sang through the air, barely missing its target. Recognition dawned in his eyes, and his lips peeled back, baring his teeth in a predatory grin. He charged at Jonathan, roaring like an angry bear.

Nancy held her breath. If the larger man could grab hold of Jonathan, he could knock the smaller man over the cliff where they fought.

Jonathan moved with a speed that took Nancy's breath. As Harpe stabbed at him with his knife, Jonathan sprang to his right and pivoted, avoiding the thrust and letting the bigger man's momentum carry him forward. Before Harpe could stop himself, Jonathan brought his arms together like scissors. His own knife sliced across Harpe's left bicep, and his tomahawk sliced through the flesh at the base of his skull. It was shallow — not a killing blow.

Harpe's enraged howl was like that of a feral beast. His knife flashed in the dim light, slicing upward, threatening to open Jonathan from belly to breastbone. Jonathan deflected the knife with his own, spun, and dealt Harpe a vicious backhand blow with his tomahawk.

The weapon gashed Harpe's right shoulder, blood soaking his sleeve. He reeled, staggering to the edge of the cliff. This time, one of Duwalla's arrows finally found its target, biting deep into the meat of Harpe's thigh. Crying out in surprise and pain, the big man teetered on the edge of the precipice. Forsaking both his knife and his tomahawk, Jonathan took a step forward and punched Harpe square in the jaw. Harpe's head snapped back, and his knife fell from his limp fingers.

He looked like a tree felled by the axe as he slowly tipped backward and vanished from sight. It seemed an eternity before he landed with a hollow thud onto the rocks below.

Nancy sobbed with relief as Jonathan drew her to her feet, cut through her bonds, and pulled her tightly against him. No words were sufficient, so they simply held one another. After a long moment, or perhaps an hour or a day — she opened her eyes and drew back so that she could look fully on his face. He was a mess, but that did not matter right now.

"You are in sore need of a bath," she said, running her hand along his dirt-coated jaw. As he stood there disheveled and unshaven, with dark circles under his eyes and his face covered in dirt, he was more handsome than ever before. She never felt more protected and more loved than she did in that moment. "I suppose it can wait until I get you back home," she whispered, stroking his cheek more gently.

Jonathan merely smiled and stared into her eyes as if he had not seen her in an eternity.

Duwalla joined them, leading Big Harpe's horse. He looked down over the cliff at the man's supine form.

"Should I go down there and make certain he is dead?" Duwalla asked.

"No. Even if he is alive, he won't be coming after us anytime soon," Jonathan said. "In fact, I almost hope he does come after me again someday. That was over entirely too fast."

Duwalla shook his head and smiled. "Jonathan Wood, you are a puzzling man. I am glad I know you."

Chapter 21

The return trip seemed to go by in a whirl. Jonathan was so relieved to have Nancy back with him, safe and unharmed, that he felt as if he were floating on the clouds. Several times he caught himself staring at her face. She was still so beautiful.

Duwalla traveled along with them at Jonathan's insistence. The Indian was aware of Nancy's discomfort with him, but if there were any hard feelings, he never let on. In fact, he went out of his way not to engage Jonathan's wife in conversation. Instead he contented himself with riding along at a respectful distance, occasionally talking with Jonathan, but otherwise remaining his quiet self.

The situation might have been more comfortable had Jonathan and Duwalla simply said their goodbyes and gone their own separate ways, but after the role he played in Nancy's rescue, there was no reason, in Jonathan's mind, for her to treat his friend with anything less than common courtesy and hospitality. For her part, Nancy remained silent and a bit distant, but she did not shy away from Duwalla nor avert her eyes when he was near.

When Duwalla had seen them safely to Moccasin Valley, they finally parted ways, with Duwalla promising to return soon. As he and Jonathan talked, Nancy busied herself with the children rather than bidding Duwalla farewell. Jonathan suspected the omission was intentional, but this was not the time to confront her about that. For now, it was enough that they were together again, a family reunited.

Late that night, they lay on a soft, bearskin rug in front of the fire, arms and legs entwined around one another, soaking up the embers' red-orange glow, and listening to the wind in the trees. He could feel her heart beat gently against his chest, and her smooth, warm skin upon his own.

"Nancy," he whispered, "I want you to know, no matter how things might have seemed in the past, that you are more important to me than anything else. If you want, we will go back East, to the New River, or Tidewater…"

"Hush," she said, lightly placing a finger across his lips. "I don't feel the way I once did. This is my home too, and I never want to leave. I mean it." She smiled and buried her face against his chest, squeezing him so tightly he thought he could not regain his breath. Just as suddenly, she let go, untangled herself from his embrace, and stood.

"I have something to give you," she whispered. She strode across the room, indifferent to her nudity, and disappeared into the back room, returning with a sheet of paper.

"It is a good thing the children are asleep," Jonathan said, eying her in a less than proper way as she sat down next to him.

"And you'd best not wake them, either," she said, her voice teasing. Nonetheless, she drew the bearskin up around them both before slipping the paper into his hands.

"What is this?" He unfolded it and held it into the firelight.

"It's the map to the mine." She took a deep breath, then continued in a rush. "I found it in Harpe's saddlebag. I know you have dreamed about finding it, and now that you no longer have your gorget, I thought…"

Jonathan cut off her words with a long, passionate kiss. Her lips were soft, her kiss firm with intent. It was like the first kiss they had ever shared. When they finally broke apart, he took a long moment before speaking.

"Duwalla once told me something about the mine," he said. "Indian legend claims that it is more than a mine, or perhaps not a mine at all. It is said there is something ancient down there. Maybe even something that should never be disturbed." He stared into the dying flames, gathering his thoughts. "It is probably not true, but in any case, I don't care about it anymore."

He balled up the paper and, before Nancy could stop him, threw it into the fire, where it set up a bright blaze for a few moments before crumpling into a black shell and finally falling apart. Needing another moment to choose his words, he added a new log to the fire. The renewed flame it sparked seemed a twin to that which was alive in his heart.

He turned to face her, cupping her chin in his hand. Surprise still registerd on her face, and her eyes were open wide. Within their depths, he could see confusion battling with relief, and hope as she waited for him to speak.

"I am sorry," he began, "that it has taken me so long to see what a rich man I truly am. I know now that I have everything I ever wanted right here."

He drew her close to him again, and they sat together in the dancing firelight. Their hearts seemed to beat as one, their very lives as entwined as their bodies. They melted together again, two souls bound together in a home made in the woods.

Epilogue

They came in silence. Hundreds, or perhaps thousands. No one seemed to agree. But they came.

They spoke to no one. In fact, they scarcely met the eye of a single person who halted in the midst of his work, or peered out her cabin door to take a look at the strange sight. Their concerns were greater than the petty lives of these people who held no love for them in any case.

They proceeded on to their sacred place—a mound from which the white man tended to shy away, as if some evil lurked beneath it. It was not so, of course. Merely superstition fed by stories told to the gullible—tales that were intended to feed into that same superstition.

It was, of course, a place of worship. It was a place where one could experience a profound sense of unity with earth, sky, and humankind. They understood that there was rapidly becoming no place for them in this part of the world, yet they held no bitterness in their hearts toward those who were slowly squeezing them out as surely as the vine chokes the flower—at least, they felt no bitterness during their time of worship.

They spoke of the creative force that made and is present in all things. They looked to the seven directions for guidance. They celebrated the Sun and Moon, who looked over the earth, and danced around the Fire, the caretaker of humankind. Fire, in turn, sent its messenger Smoke up to the heavens, carrying their supplications to the heavens. They celebrated all that bound them together as one.

They celebrated life.

When it was over, they left again in silence. They all knew their reasons for coming, and the white man had neither right to nor need of explanations, not that any would be forthcoming even should he ask.

Years later, it would be named "The Peaceful Invasion," and perhaps that is what it was.

Duwalla did not leave with the others. He was old, and his bones did not tolerate hours in the saddle as they did in his younger years. Thus, he was still not fully recovered from the trek her. Besides, there remained one more place he wanted to go.

He rode along familiar paths, noting the small changes along the way. Fewer trees, more farms, more people. He lifted his head to the unchanging mountains, where the smoke still rose, like funeral pyres in the morning sky. Jonathan once told him that the white man's Bible claimed that their god touched the mountains, and the mountains smoked. Perhaps it was true. Whatever god or gods there were, Duwalla could feel the strength of their presence among these mountains.

He guided his horse across a field, heading for a place he knew well. He did not know if those who lived here would remember him, but he hoped so. In any case, it was not them he had come to see.

He was surprised to find that someone was already there when he arrived, and was even more surprised when he saw who it was. He could not believe she still lived, but she wore her years well. She was still a strong woman.

Her eyes met his and widened in surprise, as a flicker of recognition passed through them. He nodded to her and dismounted.

Jonathan's grave was marked with only a simple stone. It seemed such a small remembrance for a life so well-lived. But Jonathan's body was with the earth, and the earth remembered all things.

A tear trickled down his cheek as he stared at his friend's final resting place.

"I miss you my friend," he said simply. "You were the best of men."

Nancy did not look at him, but she reached out and took his hand. Everything that ever stood between them melted away at that moment, and they stood united by the memory of the man they both loved. Two people lost in the memory of a life lived in the woods.

A Note from the Authors

When a work of fiction is based on a true story, it is important to separate fact from fiction. How much of this story is factual? A great deal of it, actually. We invite you to take a look at the brief biography of Jonathan's life that we have provided.

There are many areas in which we have speculated, or made changes for the sake of the story. We have no evidence that Jonathan knew Nancy Davidson prior to meeting her after the death of her husband (the story of which is factual). We have possibly placed Patrick Henry in Williamsburg a bit early in history, but not definitely. The character of Duwala is fictional. The legend of Swift's Silver Mine is real, though we have no reason to believe Jonathan ever went off in search of it, nor do we have evidence of any visits to a Melungeon settlement. We have no specific stories of Jonathan meeting up with Daniel Boone, but given the amount of time Boone spent in or passing through Moccasin Valley, it is highly unlikely that they were not acquainted. At the very least, they would have met when Boone discharged the men of Fort Houston from service.

Most of the episodes of Jonathan's life which we recount in this book are documented at least by secondary sources: The rescue of a neighbor during an Indian battle (the identity of the neighbor he saved is uncertain); Leaving the fort undefended so that the men could play "long ball" (though we never discovered how the game is played), and the women's response/prank; his participation in the battles of Island Flats and King's Mountain; even the anecdote about Edmonson being chastised for "swearing an oath" during the fighting. Jonathan did claim that he fired the shot that brought down Ferguson, (though, in fairness, so did many other men), and a musket ball truly did strike his bearskin saddle cover, causing him to fall, and leading his friends to believe he had been killed. The hanging of prisoners after King's Mountain is factual, though Jonathan's presence there is speculation based on the fact that he arrived home from King's Mountain two weeks after his neighbors.

The tale of the frontier serial killers, the Harpes, is historical fact, though their most notorious exploits came later than we have placed them in this story. Nine months after the battle of King's Mountain, the Harpes did, in fact, abduct a Susan Wood, the sister of a Frank Wood, who fought in the battle and claimed that Harpe fought on the side of the Loyalists. Nearly every character name is culled from history, though all characters are used fictitiously.

We sincerely hope you found this novella to be an entertaining way to enjoy the story of a very special man in our family's history.

Sincerely,

David Wood

David S. Wood

About the Authors

David S. Wood is a native of Scott County, Virginia, and has devoted many years to researching family history and the history of the region. A graduate of East Tennessee State University and Coastal Carolina University, David retired first from the 3M Company, and then from the University System of South Carolina. The proud father of three children, and "Pap" to six wonderful grandchildren, he now lives in Myrtle Beach, South Carolina with his wife Martha.

Okay, so they're both a little bit older now than they were in this picture.

David Wood is the author of the thriller novels *Dourado* and *Cibola*. A graduate of the University of Georgia and Walden University, David lives in the Atlanta area with his wife Cindy and their children Kyla and Erin. For more information on him and his work, visit his website at www.davidwoodweb.com.

A Brief Biography of Jonathan Wood

Jonathan Wood was born in either 1744 or 1745 in Prince William County (now Loudon County) in what was called the "Northern Neck" of Virginia. He was the son of John Wood, the third generation of the Woods, who moved from England. He worked as a surveyor for the Loyal Land Company. He met Nancy Davidson Osborne shortly after the death of her husband. They married in 1767. The exact date of their move the Moccasin Valley is uncertain, but sources tend to place it either in 1770 or 1773.

Jonathan and Nancy had four children: John, born March 25, 1771; Henry, born May 18, 1773; Jonathan, born April 23, 1778; and Polly, born February 19, 1780. Jonathan also enjoyed a close relationship with his stepson James Osborne, and later generations of their families remained allied.

During his lifetime, he served in local militias, and held offices as County Surveyor, Overseer of Roads, and Magistrate for Russell County. (The area has, at different times, been part of as Fincastle County and Washington County, and is now Scott County). He participated in many skirmishes with the natives of the region. During one particular siege by the Shawnee, he is credited with rescuing a neighbor, at great risk to himself. He served in the military under William Campbell, and fought at both the battles of Island Flats and King's Mountain. He, (along with many others) claimed to have fired the shot that brought down Major. Ferguson.

Jonathan died November 13, 1804. Nancy died on April 17, 1827.

Ancestors and Descendants of Jonathan Wood

John Wood

> Born in 1636 in England. Immigrated from London, England in 1665.
> Married in 1672. Settled in Westmoreland County where he died.

Jonathan Wood

> Born in 1675 in Westmoreland County and died there.

John Wood

> Born in 1708 in Westmoreland County. Married and moved to Loudon
> County near Leesburg. Sons: Isaac, John and Jonathan.

Jonathan Wood

> Born in 1745 in Loudon County. Married Nancy Osborne in 1767 and
> moved to Moccasin Valley approximately 1770. Died in 1804.
> Children: John, Henry, Jonathan, Molly.

Jonathan Wood

> Born in 1778 near Fort Houston. Married Ann C. Skillern approximately
> 1805. Died in 1848.   Children: Polly, William, Jonathan, James.
> *~Was involved in the formation of Scott County, Virginia. Served as
> Magistrate, Constable, and Sheriff, as well as County Surveyor.~*

Jonathan Wood

> Born in 1815. Married Sarah Jett in 1836. Died in 1889.
> Childen: James Wood, John Wood, Napoleon Bonaparte Wood, Francis
> Marion Wood, Ann Wood, Jonathan Wood, Mary Wood, Henrietta Wood.

Francis Marion Wood

> Born n 1854. Married Nancy Dorothea Welch in 1883. Died in 1918.
> Children: Dora, Myrtle, Rebecca, Elsie, Augusta, William, John, Jonathan

Jonathan Garfield Wood

> Born in 1901. Married Effie Patrick. Moved to Kingsport, Tennessee. Died
> in 1978. Children: Thelma, Betty, William Milton, Ann Lee, Harvey Howard,
> Loretta, Carolyn Sue, David.

The descendants of *Jonathan Garfield Wood* and *Effie Patrick*

Thelma Elizabeth Wood [Leon Willis]

Betty Marie Wood [Kelly C. Rhoton]
- Janice Rhoton [Dennis Long]
    - Kelly Long
- Rita Rhoton [Floyd Mann]
    - Laura Mann
- Mike Rhoton [Pam]
    - Christopher Rhoton

Ann Lee Wood [Alan Ballard]
- Kevin Ballard [Stephanie Price]
    - Jason Ballard
    - Meghan Ballard
- Robin Ballard [Mary Tilton]
    - Sarah Ballard
    - Uriah Ballard
    - Rachel Ballard
    - Ronnie Ballard
- Tessie Ballard [Greg Scurei]
    - Erica Scurei
    - Christopher Scurei
    - David Scurei
    - Bradley Scurei
- Sue Ballard [Daryl Groleau]
    - Cara Ballard
- Jackie Ballard [Anthony Aillet]
    - Isabel Aillet
    - Justin Aillet
    - Jaron Aillet
- John Ballard [Jill Frazier]
    - Savanna Ballard
    - Emily Rose Ballard
    - Brooklyn Ballard

William Milton Wood [Joan Adams]
- Jonathan Mark Wood [Michelle O'Neal]
  - Jonathan Devin Wood
- Neva Gail Wood [Harry Ennis]
  - Emily Ennis
  - Leah Ennis

Harvey Howard Wood [Shirley Faye Cassel]
- Marianne Wood [Scott Hanna] *[Child from first marriage]*
  - Matthew Terrell
- David Scott Wood II
- Paul Harvey Wood

Loretta Wood [James Muse]
- Sharon Elizabeth Muse [Barry Sasser]
  - Samantha Morgan Sasser
- James William Muse [Debra Elizabeth Yarbrough]
  - Amanda Elizabeth Muse

Carolyn Sue Wood [Samuel Hall]
- Lisa Hall

David Scott Wood [Martha Kenneally]
[Children from first marriage to Barbara Debord]
- David Benjamin Wood [Cynthia Shaw]
  - Kyla Wood
  - Erin Wood
- Lee Ann Wood [Robert Gourlay]
  - Brett Gourlay
  - Samuel Gourlay
- Cynthia Marie Wood [Thomas Baker]
  - Alexis Baker
  - Katherine Baker

The authors gratefully acknowledge the following resources which provided either specific details, or general information.

Addington, Omer C., *History of Scott County, Vol. II*- No publisher or publication date available.

Addington, Robert M., *History of Scott County, Virginia,* 1932, Privately Printed

Draper, Lyman C., *King's Mountain and its Heroes*, 1996, The Overmountain Press, Johnson City, TN

Elder, Pat Spurlock, *Melungeons: Examining an Appalachian Legend*, 1999, Continuity Press, Blountville, TN

Fischer, David Hackett, *Albion's Seed,* 1989, Oxford University Press, New York, NY

Hammon, Neal O., *My Father, Daniel Boone- The Draper Interviews with Nathan Boone*, 1999, The University Press of Kentucky, Lexington, KY

Hawke, David Freeman, *Everyday Life in Early America, 1988,* HarperCollins, New York, NY

Heath, Craig L., *The Virginia Papers- Volume 1: Volume 1ZZ of the Draper Manuscript Collection,2006,* Heritage Books, Westminster, MD

Hines, Emilee, It *Happened in Virginia,* 2001, The Globe Pequot Press, Guilford, CT

Holt, Michael F., *The Rise and Fall of the American Whig Party*, 1999, Oxford University Press, New York, NY

Jones, Randall, *In the Footsteps of Daniel Boone*, 2005, John F. Blair, Winston-Salem, NC

Kennedy, Billy, *The Scots-Irish in the Hills of Tennessee,* 1995, Causeway Press, Belfast

Kennedy, N. Brent & Kennedy, Robyn Vaughan, *The Melungeons: The Resurrection of a Proud People*, 1997, Mercer University Press, Macon, GA

Leyburn, James G., *The Scotch-Irish, A Social History*, 1962, The University of North Carolina Press, Chapel Hill, NC

Lofaro, Michael A., *The Life and Adventures of Daniel Boone,* 1986, The University Press of Kentucky, Lexington, KY

Morgan, Robert, *Boone: A Biography,* 2007, Algonquin Books of Chapel Hill, Chapel Hill, NC

Morison, Hon. H.S.K., Virginia Law Register, January 1904, Vol. 9

Randall, Willard Sterne, *Washington: A Life*, 1997, Henry Holt and Company, New York, NY

Sloane, Eric, *Sketches of America Past*, 1986, Promontory Press, New York, NY

Summers, Lewis Preston, *History of Southwest Virginia 1746-1786, Washington County 1777-1780,* 1903/1989, The Overmountain Press, Johnson City, TN

Thwaites, Reuben Gold & Kellogg, Louise Phelps, *Documentary History of Dunmore's War 1774, Compiled from the Draper Manuscripts,* 1905, Wisconsin Historical Society, Madison, WI

Wood, M.B., History of the wood Family in Virginia: *A Brief Account of the Wood Family in Virginia containing A Short Memoir of James O. Wood and his Ancestors from their Earliest Settlement in the Colony of Virginia to his Death,* J.B. Lippincott Co., Philadelphia, 1893